"Would it be ... to be a real wife?"

Clarry blushed at her husband's question and could only whisper her reply. "Yes, yes it would. The fact that I had a foolish crush on you most of my life doesn't mean I could . . . I could do that."

"If you recall," Rob spoke evenly, "we didn't start out like this. It was your idea we have this kind of marriage."

Clarry looked away and muttered, "That was because I didn't know then that you didn't love me. At least, not as a man loves a woman."

"Unfortunately, you weren't quite a woman at the time."

"But we can't go on like this for the rest of our lives, Rob!" Clarry protested. "I'm not a child anymore!"

"Then it's up to you to prove it." Rob's response was curt, and she saw a kind of anger in his eyes she'd never seen before.

Lindsay Armstrong married an accountant from New Zealand and settled down—if you can call it that—in Australia. A coast-to-coast camping trip later, they moved to a six-hundred-acre mixed-grain property, which they eventually abandoned to the mice and leeches and black flies. Then, after a winning career at the track with an untried trotter, purchased "mainly because he had blue eyes," they opted for a more conventional family life with their five children in Brisbane, where Lindsay now writes.

Books by Lindsay Armstrong

Don't miss any of our special offers. Write to us at the following address for information on our newest releases.

Harlequin Reader Service
901 Fuhrmann Blvd., P.O. Box 1397, Buffalo, NY 14240
Canadian address: P.O. Box 603,
Fort Erie, Ont. L2A 5X3

The Heart of the Matter

Lindsay Armstrong

Harlequin Books

TORONTO • NEW YORK • LONDON
AMSTERDAM • PARIS • SYDNEY • HAMBURG
STOCKHOLM • ATHENS • TOKYO • MILAN

Original hardcover edition published in 1987
by Mills & Boon Limited

ISBN 0-373-02876-8

Harlequin Romance first edition December 1987
Second printing November 1987

CHAPTER ONE

CLARISSA RANDALL stared out of her bedroom window over the historic acres of Mirrabilla but didn't see the dun gold grass of the winter paddocks, the mobs of sheep or the dark blue-green of the gum trees that lined the meandering path of Mirrabilla Creek as it wound towards the horizon.

Instead, in her mind's eye, she saw a montage of her close family, past and present. Her beloved but remote father; her brother Ian—so young; her exceptionally beautiful mother; Sophie ... And Robert Randall with his dark good looks and his curiously dynamic yet at the same time withdrawn personality.

Something of an enigma, she had once heard his father say of Rob. And in her youthful heart she had pondered this, not to know how many years later she would still be pondering it.

She sighed suddenly and came out of her reverie. As she turned away from the window she was conscious of an odd, very slight prickling of her skin, and wondered why it should be doing that. But her silent bedroom yielded no answer and her thoughts slid away to something more concrete—such as what she'd let herself in for on this cold, bright winter's day.

Horizons was a weekly television programme that featured different Australian lifestyles, places of historic interest, people of interest, and when the request had come, asking Clarissa for an interview and footage on Mirrabilla, her first inclination had been to decline.

But she'd shown the letter to Rob and he had thought otherwise. 'But I'm not of any interest to anyone,' she'd said with a grimace. He had raised a dark eyebrow at her and murmured that the Kingstons of Mirrabilla had always been of interest to other Australians. Then he'd added that of course if she didn't feel up to it, not to worry about it.

Which had the immediate effect, she thought ruefully, of making me insist that I was perfectly able to handle it and of writing back that same day to Moira Stapleton to accept. Then, just as I was getting quite interested in sorting through all the old papers and memorabilia I could find, Sophie got that nasty virus, which is how I got myself landed with Evonne Patterson, press secretary, PR lady extraordinaire and I don't what else . . .

Her thoughts were broken at that point by a tap on the door. She just knew it was Evonne and forcibly restrained herself from saying—speak of the devil!

She called instead, 'Come in!'

Evonne Patterson came in with her usual model's walk and restrained smile. She was about twenty-six— several years older than Clarissa—but despite looking and dressing like a model, and possessing great dark eyes and an unusually pale skin, she was, Clarissa knew, extremely efficient at her job. One of the reasons Clarissa was so sure of this was simply that Rob would not tolerate anything less.

Which is why she's in my bedroom now, Clarissa reminded herself. Apart from Sophie's virus, she's here on Rob's behalf, I just *know* to make sure nothing goes wrong. I just wish she didn't make me feel—slow and dull, sometimes.

'The crew has arrived, Mrs Randall,' Evonne said. 'Oh. Oh, very nice,' she went on as she eyed Clarissa critically. 'Mr Randall would approve, I'm sure, although . . .' She broke off in mid-sentence.

Clarissa waited for a moment as those large dark eyes were narrowed thoughtfully. She was actually an inch or so taller than Evonne Patterson, but had often found it was no advantage—unless feeling like a leggy colt could be called advantageous.

'You were going to say?' she asked.

'I just wondered if your hair would be better up—I mean, it looks very nice,' Evonne said slowly. 'But for the outside shots—well, it's a bit windy.'

Clarissa turned to her dressing table mirror and encountered an unusually stubborn look in her eyes which at first startled and then amused her. *Didn't know I could look like that . . .!* However, there's no point in being stubborn for stubborn's sake, as Mrs Jacobs would say!

She looked at herself equally critically in the glass. She had chosen, after much heart-searching, to wear a soft, misty-grey tweed pantsuit. The jacket was beautifully tailored and rather like a man's hacking jacket, and there was a matching waistcoat which she wore over a cornflower blue, finest pure wool sweater with several fine gold chains of varying lengths. A pair of black patent leather pumps with little heels completed the outfit. *Not too dressy, she'd decided, but dressy enough to show that I'm the lady of the manor, which is what I'm supposed to be portraying, I presume, and practical. But to get back to the point in question . . .*

She pushed her hands into the pockets of her jacket and swung her head so that her long, streaky-fair hair swung out. It came to well below her shoulders and it settled into a shining, springy but well-mannered curtain.

My best asset? she pondered, examining her slightly darker eyebrows, golden skin which would never be dramatically pale and her blue-grey eyes which didn't flash magnificently but did have rather long thick, curving lashes.

Yes, she decided, my best asset—why is it that Evonne always makes me feel insipid as well as everything else? As if I blend rather well into the winter landscape?

'Perhaps you could just tie it back, Mrs Randall?'

Clarissa closed her left eyelid in the barest wink at her reflection and turned from the mirror. 'I think I'll just leave it,' she said tranquilly. 'I never feel really comfortable with my hair up.'

'Well, tied back ...'

'Or tied back,' Clarissa said evenly. Which was not altogether true because she frequently wore it tied back, but it seemed important to take a stand about something. But she managed to smile at Evonne Patterson.

For which effort she received an unusually warm smile in return. 'Of course you're *right*,' Evonne said ruefully. 'It's so beautiful it's a pity to hide it—I was only thinking of the practicalities, but one can go through life being too practical, can't one?' She shrugged quizzically and smoothed her scarlet suit which she wore with a black blouse.

Clarissa stared at her and discovered that she'd had the wind taken right out of her sails—but not only that, she now felt as if she was being vain about her hair. How does she do it? she wondered. *Why* does she do it, or is it my imagination?

She turned away and bit her lip and counted to ten beneath her breath. And thought, it probably is my imagination—rendered even more fanciful than usual this morning because I'm suddenly terrified about this interview, I think. Why on earth did I agree to it? Who knows what could come out, I never thought of that. What *did* I think, apart from being foolishly goaded into it by what Rob said? That it might be a . . . a sort of tribute to my father and Ian because they'd loved Mirrabilla so much?

She took a deep breath and turned back to Evonne. 'I gather Miss Stapleton isn't here yet?'

'No. She's travelling independently of the crew, apparently.' Evonne grinned suddenly. 'They call her Cleopatra behind her back—I overheard them.'

'Do they?' Clarissa grimaced. 'I think I'd better have a cup of coffee, then, while I've still got the time, to fortify me!'

'You'll be just fine, Mrs Randall,' Evonne assured her. 'Er . . . what about Sophie?'

'Clover has taken her into Holbrook with him to do a few errands. She doesn't need to be here for it all.'

'Oh. About the dress I suggested . . .?'

Clarissa directed a very firm glance at Evonne Patterson. 'I thought it was too dressy for Sophie,' she said calmly, however. 'I've told Mrs Jacobs what she's to wear. Will you join me for a cup of coffee, Evonne?'

'Thank you.' Evonne Patterson glanced at her long scarlet nails that exactly matched her glossy lips and scarlet suit, and added, 'By the way, Mr Randall rang while you were showering. He asked me to tell you that he might be home later today, after all.'

'Oh, I do hope so!' Clarissa replied.

Moira Stapleton, who was the compère and one of the producers of *Horizons*, was beautiful, Clarissa decided. Golden-blonde, very chic and not at all Cleopatra-like. She also had a reputation for integrity as a television journalist, in fact a very high reputation, which made it something of an honour to be featured on her programme.

But after a while, Clarissa could see where the Cleopatra bit came from. For although she was warm and friendly, she was also utterly decisive and very persuasive. Which was how Clarissa came to change into riding gear and do a sequence herding sheep with her favourite black and white border collie, Mem.

'After all,' Moira had said, 'sheep are what Mirrabilla is essentially about, aren't they? Over the years—many, many years—the Kingstons have built up a most respected flock of merinos. Besides which, Mrs Randall,' she had added quietly, 'I want to capture the essential *you*, as the last of the Kingstons and doing something which I believe you love.'

Clarissa had hesitated and wondered how she'd dug that out.

'I did mention that we would want something of this nature to Miss Patterson,' Moira had said then.

A tiny silence had fallen and for once Evonne had suddenly looked acutely uncomfortable.

'All right,' Clarissa had said. 'Give me a few minutes. I'm afraid with Sophie being ill, Evonne was seconded in at the last minute to take over at this end. We probably had a crossed wire ...' And she'd wondered why she was making excuses for Evonne Patterson, for that matter why Evonne had made no mention of this, but in the rush to get changed because they were already on a tight schedule, she didn't have time to ponder it further.

In fact it was only over lunch that she thought of it again. Mrs Jacobs, who had been at Mirrabilla for as long as Clarissa could remember and who proudly held the dual roles of housekeeper and nanny, had set up a buffet on the verandah which seemed to be warmly appreciated by everyone.

But as Clarissa ate, Evonne appeared to be anxious to make up for what had happened in the morning, and with every bite she took, Clarissa could feel that anxiety until Evonne suggested, 'You'll probably need to take a shower, Mrs Randall, as well as get changed. Should we . . .?'

'Don't tell me I'm looking windblown, because I know it,' Clarissa said with a laugh, and was surprised to see Evonne colour faintly.

'I just wish I could look as gorgeously windblown as you can, Mrs Randall,' Moira Stapleton put in. 'I guess we'll all need brushing up, but we don't need to bolt this delicious lunch.'

'What about Sophie?' Evonne said then, apparently restored to normal and with an interrogative look at Clarissa.

'Mrs Jacobs will take care of her, Evonne,' Clarissa said steadily, and neither of them noticed the slightly curious look Moira Stapleton cast them.

'. . . Mrs Randall, I did explain to you that the sequence we've done things in is not necessarily how the final show will appear—we often interpose and cut backwards and forwards, and it's quite possible that the chat we're about to have will be broken into segments.'

'Yes, I understand,' said Clarissa. She was showered and back in her pantsuit and her hair gleamed and rippled.

Moira Stapleton smiled at her. 'You've been terrific so far. And it was a marvellous tour of the property you took us on. As for you on horseback——!'

'Thank you,' smiled Clarissa.

'So now I thought we might discuss your background and then do a tour of the house and its treasures.' They were sitting in the drawing-room and Moira Stapleton glanced at her crew. They came to attention and she turned back to Clarissa and bowed her head briefly. 'Mrs Randall, you were born here at Mirrabilla, weren't you? A direct descendant of the first Bernard Kingston who came to Australia in the eighteen-fifties to find his fortune.'

'That's right. He came to look for gold, actually, and spent some years prospecting in the Ballarat and Bendigo fields—with no success, though, so he turned his attention to sheep. And for some time he was a jack of all trades—drover, shearer, wool classer in places as far apart as Wilcannia and the Diamantina, as you'll see from his diary.'

'So he acquired a great knowledge not only about sheep but outback, eastern Australia, and not only *that*, being an educated man, kept a diary?'

'Yes. But as well as a great knowledge, he also had a great love of the bush. In fact, if he hadn't met my great-great-grandmother and if his elder brother hadn't died unexpectedly and with no heirs, he might have spent his life wandering. But he married Lucy Winthrop and took her back to England, where he sold up most of what he'd inherited and with the money, came back and bought up Mirrabilla.'

'Why this area particularly, Mrs Randall? Do you know?'

'He loved the Murray River and the Snowy Mountains, and this is fairly close to both.'

'It was also a very astute buy—this area is home to some of the world's largest sheep studs,' Moira Stapleton said. 'And this in fact is the original homestead?'

'Well, it's been added to over the years.'

'And it looks to be in excellent condition—and so picturesque, not to mention enormous!'

'It's been fairly recently renovated,' Clarissa told her, glancing up at the high ceiling. 'But basically it's astonishingly sound considering how old some parts of it are.'

'Why did you look up at the ceiling?' asked Moira.

'Well, the original one in here was a pressed iron one with lovely mouldings that I used to know off by heart, almost. Unfortunately, it had rusted in parts and we finally had to replace it. I'm still not used to the new one.'

'You love Mirrabilla, don't you, Mrs Randall? I should imagine your great-great-grandfather would be happy to know you were here, and so caught up and conversant with the running of it, as you demonstrated this morning. Your mother,' Moira Stapleton went on, changing tack fluently, 'came from Melbourne as a very young bride and was a great socialite, wasn't she?'

'Yes.'

Moira smiled. 'I didn't mean that in a frivolous sense. I believe she raised a great deal of money for charity. Do you take after her at all?'

'Not in looks. Not so far in socialising,' Clarissa answered.

'Do you remember any of the great parties she gave here at Mirrabilla?'

'Oh yes. It wasn't so long ago.'

'No. Do you miss her since she remarried and went to live in America?'

'Naturally. And I miss my father.'

'It's—fairly common knowledge,' Moira Stapleton

said delicately, 'that Mirrabilla was nearly lost to the Kingston family recently.'

'Yes, it was,' Clarissa agreed. 'My grandfather, my father's father, was killed in the Second World War. My father was too young to take over and my grandmother was quite devastated, so Mirrabilla went rather badly downhill. And when he was old enough, my father was faced with the task of building it up again through a difficult period for wool generally that affected even breeders. And while we were still weathering that, my brother Ian was killed in an air crash. My father was never really the same afterwards, and he himself died several years later.'

'Leaving only you.'

'And my mother.'

'Of course. But let's move on from that painful part.' Moira Stapleton said tactfully, and smiled at her. 'Because in fact all was not lost, was it? It's also fairly common knowledge that there was a Prince Charming waiting in the wings, although in disguise. But perhaps you'd like to tell us about your romance with Robert Randall? Starting from the time he worked here.'

'Oh,' Clarissa heard herself saying lightly, somewhat to her amazement, 'he didn't actually work here, although he helped out. His father was studmaster here for twenty years and naturally Rob lived here too.'

'So you've known him all your life?'

'Yes.' Clarissa hesitated and then smiled. 'I believe I asked him to marry me when I was about six! He taught me to ride my first pony and I thought he was utterly wonderful, even though he kept making me get straight back on every time I fell off.'

'What did he say to your proposal?'

'He said we'd have to wait until I was grown up and by then I'd probably have changed my mind.'

'Which you never did,' Moira said warmly.

'No.'

'But you were not to know—neither was he, for that matter—that he was heir to a great fortune. That his grandfather was in fact Robert T. Randall?'

'No. It came as a great surprise to all of us,' Clarissa told her, and when Moira Stapleton looked at her expectantly, she went on, 'Except Rob's father, of course.'

'Do tell us!'

'Well, Rob's father and his grandfather fell out. I think they were both rather eccentric in their own ways, but it was a major rift and they never forgave each other. And it was only when Rob's father died that my father found two letters amongst his papers— one addressed to him explaining about Robert T. Randall and asking him to get in touch with him, and one addressed to Rob himself.'

'And in the course of time,' Moira Stapleton put in, 'he was able to put Mirrabilla back on its feet, at the same time ensuring that a part of the Kingston family would still be here. That's a tremendous story, Mrs Randall! Thank you for sharing it with us . . . Cut! It really was,' she said, turning back to Clarissa. 'And I appreciate the way you told it—just simply and honestly. I was thinking now . . . oh!' She looked away as the drawing-room door opened and a very small girl advanced cautiously into the room and then raced over to Clarissa. 'Well,' said Moira, 'who might this be—no, don't tell me. Sophie Randall, and right on cue!'

Sophie Randall was a dazzling blonde with very blue eyes and just two years old—and, like the basically healthy child she was, had recovered almost miraculously from her virus. But it was some time before she could be persuaded to lift her face from her mother's shoulder and smile for the cameras. In fact it took the combined efforts of two cameramen, who became galvanised into portraying Donald Duck and Mickey Mouse to do it.

'If you ask me, Mrs Randall,' Moira Stapleton said laughingly as she eyed the antics of the crew, 'Sophie is going to be a real heartbreaker. She's already a slayer of grown men!'

'You're not wrong,' Clarissa agreed ruefully, and then both she and Sophie lifted their heads and went still. Sophie put her little hand on Clarissa's cheek and said to her joyfully, 'Daddy come!'

'Sounds like it, darling.'

Whereupon Sophie wriggled off her lap and raced out on to the verandah in a flash of blue dungarees.

'Well, this is a surprise,' said Moira Stapleton. 'I take it Mr Randall has arrived?'

'He said he might,' said Clarissa.

'Super!' Moira Stapleton smiled some time later. 'We didn't expect you, Mr Randall, but I know it will be an added plus for the programme. And that last shot of the three of you just caps it off. You have a very lovely, charming wife—she's been superb today! And as for your daughter . . .'

'I can imagine,' Robert Randall said with a grin and Sophie's hand tucked into his. He had just released Clarissa.

'I'll let you know well in advance when this segment goes to air. Goodbye, all!'

They waved Moira Stapleton off, and then her crew in their Range Rover.

'She doesn't believe in fraternising,' Robert Randall observed.

'No. They call her Cleopatra. But I thought she was very nice,' Clarissa said huskily.

'It sounds as if it was a great success, as if you two wowed them. Only,' he stopped and searched her face critically, 'you're looking a bit pale now, Clarry.'

Clarissa raised her blue-grey eyes to her tall, dark husband's very blue ones. 'Just glad it's over,' she said quietly.

'If it was going to be a strain you shouldn't . . .'

'No!' she broke in. 'I'm fine, and I'm glad I did it.'

'Come inside, then, and I'll pour you a drink.' He picked Sophie up. 'Nearly supper time for you, little one, I guess.'

'Bath time first,' Mrs Jacobs said firmly, materialising beside them, and Sophie, who adored her bath, went off with her quite happily.

'Er . . .' Evonne cleared her throat from the shadows of the verandah behind them.

Robert Randall turned to her. 'You're not planning to go home tonight, are you, Evonne?'

'I was, actually,' said Evonne. 'I've spent two nights here already and I wouldn't like to wear out my welcome.' She smiled faintly. 'But I didn't expect it to finish so late. However, I can put up in Holbrook for the night.'

Rob said, 'That's ridiculous!' And looked at Clarissa.

'Of course you must stay the night, Evonne,' Clarissa told her. 'It's only good sense. Anyway, we'd enjoy having your company for dinner,' she added after a slight pause during which she was struck by the oddest impression that there was something curiously unguarded and vulnerable in Evonne's dark eyes.

Perhaps she's afraid I'll tell Rob about that little mix-up we had this morning? The fleeting thought touched her mind, together with a twinge of uncertainty about Evonne Patterson. 'Do stay,' she said then, more warmly, and wasn't quite sure why.

They ate formally because Mrs Jacobs had insisted on setting the long, gleaming mahogany table in the dining-room, and her meal was a masterpiece—a creamy mushroom soup, homemade, a hearty oxtail casserole for which she was renowned, followed by fruit and cheese.

Nor was the meal marred by hidden tensions as Clarissa had been afraid it might. But then when Rob set his mind to charm and put people at their ease, he was usually successful, and he soon had both Clarissa and Evonne recounting incidents of the day with some hilarity.

So much so that only a very small portion of Clarissa's mind remained tuned in to the effect Evonne might have on Rob and vice versa. Not, she did acknowledge to herself, that she would be able to tell what Rob was thinking. But, she also acknowledged, there was nothing in Evonne's manner that indicated anything more than the way most females reacted to the dynamic, handsome enigma that was Robert Randall. Nor was the dynamism much in evidence tonight, she reflected, as she watched Rob lying back in his chair, sipping his wine and dropping the odd idle remark into the conversation. He's so . . . I don't know what, she thought with a sudden pang. He's got both of us eating out of his hand right at this moment . . .

'. . . Sorry! What was that?' She turned to Evonne. 'I was saying that you were so good with those sheep, you and Mem. I always thought they were exceptionally silly creatures. And the way you rode that horse! As if you were born in the saddle.'

'Thank you. But that was only a small mob . . .'

'Clarissa is one of the best riders and drovers I've ever seen,' said Rob, and smiled lazily at her.

'Only because you taught me so well,' she assured him, but couldn't help colouring faintly with pleasure. 'Shall we take our coffee in the drawing-room?' she added almost immediately.

'I'm glad I did stay after all,' commented Evonne from in front of the huge fireplace. 'It's been a nice way to wind down. Thank you both.'

'It has, hasn't it?' Clarissa agreed, and was conscious again of a feeling of confusion regarding Evonne Patterson. Because she had been good company and shown no desire to be upstaging, nor had she and Rob talked business as well they might have—she was his press secretary, after all. Maybe it was just my overwrought imagination this morning, she mused.

Then Evonne yawned delicately and said she thought she might go to bed. '. . . You don't have to come with me, Mrs Randall. I know my way. I'll just have to unpack some things,' she said whimsically.

'Oh,' Clarissa smiled at her, 'I don't mind. I can check that you have everything you need.'

But of course everything was perfect in the guestroom because Mrs Jacobs was another of those superefficient people, and if there was one thing Clarissa's mother had been able to imbue in her daughter, it was correct hostessing procedures.

In fact, escorting Evonne Patterson to bed reminded Clarissa of her mother, and as she walked back down the passageway lined with oil paintings of her

Kingston ancestors, she wondered who her mother was entertaining now in her Malibu house or maybe the Palm Springs one. But whichever, there would be someone staying, unless she had changed drastically over the past months, or her ultra-wealthy American husband had changed her . . .

Rob was still stretched out in his favourite chair before the fire when Clarissa walked back into the drawing-room, but he looked round as her heels tapped on the parquet floor. 'Set for the night?' he asked.

'Yes.' Clarissa stopped beside his chair. 'I think I'll go to bed too. I am tired now.'

He stood up. 'I've got a few things to go over . . .'

He looked down at her, then put a hand on her shoulder and tipped her chin up with his other hand. 'All right?' he queried quietly but with those blue eyes curiously probing.

'Yes,' she whispered, and felt that odd prickle again.

He stared down at her until she said, 'I am really, Rob.'

'Good.' He released her chin and bent to kiss her brow. 'Sleep well, Clarry.'

'I made it,' Clarissa said out loud to herself as she closed the bedroom door and leant back against it briefly. Then she pushed herself away and started on the familiar routine of getting herself ready for bed.

It was a huge room with a magnificent double four-poster bed, its own fireplace and a muted colour scheme of avocado green, ivory and pink copied from the beautiful and very old chintz curtains.

Yes, I made it, she mused as she changed into a fine Vyella nightgown with delicate pintucking and frills round the neck and wrists. And she went to sleep with that thought on her mind and with the shadows of the flames from the fire flickering on the ivory wallpaper.

But when she woke, the room was cold and dark and she tensed, coming wide awake in an instant with the day rushing back at her in the clearest detail. And she suddenly knew that she hadn't made it at all, that she'd only been fooling herself—that Rob had been right, the strain of it or something, had been too much.

'Oh God, oh God!' she whispered with her knuckles pressed to her mouth. But the tears started to flow and she sat up and hugged herself distraughtly, with her hair falling over her face. Then she reached for the glass of water on the table beside the bed, but knocked it over and froze as it thumped on to the carpet and then rolled off noisily on to the floor.

Please don't let him hear, she prayed. Please . . .

But the interleading door opened and she saw the tall figure of Robert Randall outlined in the light from the next bedroom. Then a switch clicked and her own room was flooded with light.

Rob was still dressed but wearing a navy-blue sweater instead of his jacket and his dark hair was ruffled as if he had run his fingers through it recently. He said interrogatively, 'Clarry? What's wrong?'

'N-nothing,' she stammered.

'So why are you crying?'

'I . . . I . . .' She put her hands to her face as if to hide the evidence.

'Oh yes, you are.' He came over to the bed and sat down beside her.

'I'm cold. I mean that's not why, but I should have built up the fire. I mean . . .' She tailed off incoherently.

'You mean,' he said after a moment, 'the day was

too much for you.'

'No! I'm not an invalid! Why should it have been too much? I'm as strong as a horse.' But the tears were streaming down her face again and he made an impatient sound and pulled her into his arms.

'Tell me why you're so upset, then!' he commanded, and smoothed her tangled hair away from her face.

Clarissa stared up at him with her lips set mutinously, but he smudged her tears with his fingers and a few last strands of hair from the corner of her mouth, and said, 'Clarry.'

She closed her eyes and turned her face into the navy-blue wool of his jumper. Because, for almost as long as she could remember anything, she could remember Rob Randall saying 'Clarry' to her in just that tone of voice. Quietly, but in a way that brooked no defiance, that told her it was useless to try to evade him.

'I . . . all those *lies* I told today,' she wept. 'All the false images I presented—*we* did! Happy family, happy wife . . .'

CHAPTER TWO

ROB was silent until Clarissa's tears subsided and she turned her face back to him and sniffed miserably.

Then he seemed to sigh, and reached for the cobweb-fine, lacy shawl that lay across the bottom of the bed and wrapped her in its voluminous folds, pulled the pillows up and laid her back against them. He stood up and walked across to the fireplace where he picked up the poker and with the aid of some kindling and logs from the basket on the hearth, got it going again. He came back to the bed, wiping his hands on his handkerchief, then bent down and retrieved the fallen glass. Then he sat down beside her again.

'It was your idea that we have this kind of marriage,' he said evenly, at last. 'We didn't start out like this, if you recall.'

Clarissa had watched his every move, her eyes huge and dark. She looked away now and muttered, 'That was because I didn't know . . .'

'There are a lot of things you don't know, Clarry,' he interrupted.

'I do know you didn't love me,' she whispered. 'Not the way—the proper way for a man and a woman.'

'Unfortunately, you weren't quite a woman.'

'I was old enough to have Sophie.'

'That's a biological matter,' he said drily. 'But otherwise, to have reacted the way you did . . .'

'How else should I have reacted?' she said agitatedly.

He watched her carefully for a moment and then shrugged slightly. 'All right, if you don't want to talk about it, if it still upsets you so much . . .'

'No, I don't want to talk about it—that. And not because it upsets me,' Clarissa said with a sudden spark of anger in her eyes, 'but because it can't change anything. It happened and that's that. I just don't understand *why* you want me to live with you as a dutiful little wife when you wouldn't ever have married me if . . . if . . .' She stopped abruptly at the ironic glance he cast her, and felt herself flushing.

'Would it be so very hard to be a real wife?' he queried after a moment.

'Yes—yes, it would,' she whispered, and licked her lips. 'The fact that I had a foolish crush on you for most of my life doesn't mean I could . . . I could do that.'

'Then what we have is the only alternative, Clarry. I thought, as a matter of fact, I thought you were happy—content, anyway. You're doing what you like best now, just as you dreamt of when you were a teenager. You always said you wanted to help run Mirrabilla.'

She was silent and he watched her pleating the cream wool of the shawl a little feverishly. And when she gave no sign of answering, his mouth hardened and he said, 'I must warn you, Clarry, if you're thinking of trying to run away again, don't.'

'But we can't go on like this for the rest of our lives, Rob!'

'That's up to you,' he said curtly.

'Rob . . .'

'Clarry, if you think I'd let not one but two children loose in the world, you're mistaken.'

'Oh, Rob,' she protested, her eyes agonised, 'I'm not

a child any more. I'm twenty-*two*.'

'Then prove it,' he said.

'I . . .' Clarissa's voice stuck in her thoat and she flinched at his brief, cold smile. Then she struck out blindly with words. 'Isn't your revenge complete otherwise, Rob? But then aren't you hurting yourself as much as anyone?'

He had been looking down, but his dark lashes lifted abruptly and she saw the kind of anger in his eyes she had never seen directed at *her* before. Not even when she'd run away. Then it was gone, to be replaced by a sort of mild cynicism, and he said quite gently, 'If I'd really set my mind to it, Clarry, I could have come up with something *much* better in that line. Such as seeing you evicted from here or sold off to the highest bidder. Take James Halliday, for example.' He paused as she bit her lip. 'I imagine,' he went on dispassionately, 'you would have found being taken to his bed first, instead of mine, not quite what you would have liked. I imagine he would have left that lovely soft, very young body of yours,' his blue gaze flickered down and then up again meaningfully, 'rather bruised and hurt, don't you think? Which you have to acquit me of at least, in spite of all my other— sins. I don't suppose he would have cared much that you were extremely innocent and—frightened.'

Clarissa took a faltering breath and tried to look away, but something in his gaze wouldn't let her. 'No,' she whispered at last, 'he wouldn't have. Oh, Rob, it's not that I don't . . . appreciate that . . .' She put a hand to her mouth. 'I sometimes don't know *what* to think, you know.'

They sat like that for a while, in silence, but Clarissa had managed to look away at last.

'Why don't you think of Sophie, then?' he said

eventually, and his voice was quite different and the cynical light had gone out of his eyes. 'And how much it would hurt all of us if we subjected her to a custody battle.'

'Yes, of course . . .'

Robert touched her hot cheek with his fingers and his voice was different again as he said, 'I've got an even better idea. Why don't you forget all about it and try to sleep now? Shall I get you a hot drink?'

'. . . No, thanks. I'll be fine.' She tried to smile.

'You said that earlier.'

'I . . .' She made an enormous effort to stop her voice from wobbling. 'Perhaps I just needed to get it off my chest. You're up very late, aren't you?'

'I was just coming to bed. It's only,' he glanced at his watch and raised his eyebrows, 'it's one o'clock, later than I thought.'

'Why do you still work so hard?' she asked involuntarily.

He shrugged. 'Habit, I guess. But there are times when I find it hard to sleep too. Goodnight, Clarry.'

She stared at the door he'd left slightly ajar until his light went out as well and there was only the firelight in the room, flickering and casting odd shadows. And she turned her cheek to the pillow and found herself looking back over the years, to when she had been very young . . .

'. . . Clarissa Jane Kingston! Oh, look at you! Dirty and *torn*—little boys might get around like that, but not little girls!'

'I don't think Clarry knows the difference yet,' Ian Kingston said with all the wisdom of his fourteen years as opposed to Clarissa's six.

'Do so!' Clarissa objected.

'Now look here, Master Ian,' Mrs Jacobs intervened hastily, 'you shouldn't encourage her . . .'

'*Encourage* her!' It was Ian's turn to object. 'That's the last thing I do. Why would I want a kid sister tagging along wherever I go? She *follows* us whenever she gets the chance. Maybe we ought to build her a doll's house—and lock her in! I mean, she nearly drowned the other day. We didn't even know she was there until we heard her cry out, and there she was, upstream, sailing into the creek on the end of a rod.'

'But I caught that fish,' Clarissa said proudly. 'Didn't I, Ian? Rob said it was a beauty.'

'*It* caught *you*,' Ian replied loftily. 'The thing is, you know you're not allowed down at the creek, Clarry.'

'I am with you and Rob . . .'

'But we didn't take you! You followed when you were supposed to be doing something else.'

'What she needs are some kids of her own age,' Mrs Jacobs said worriedly. 'She's got—twenty-six dolls!'

'But I like horses,' Clarissa said candidly. 'Not dolls. And fishing and swimming . . .'

'We do know that,' her brother broke in sarcastically. 'Anyway, Rob's teaching her to ride—that's why she's in such a mess today, so don't blame me for it, Mrs Jacobs. For some reason he has more patience with her.'

'Well, your father did agree that she could learn—heaven help us, but I still don't see why she should be in such a mess.'

'I fell off. Into a puddle . . .'

'It was soft mud,' said Ian as Mrs Jacobs began to feel Clarissa's limbs anxiously.

'But . . .'

'Everyone falls off, Mrs Jacobs, but you can trust Rob to see that she doesn't hurt herself. And old

Cuddles is as safe as houses.'

'It was my fault,' Clarissa said earnestly. 'Rob said I was daydreaming.'

About nine months later, on the morning of her seventh birthday, Clarissa said softly, 'Oh . . .' and started to cry.

Ian Kingston and Rob Randall looked at each other ruefully. It was a beautiful summery morning during the first week of the school holidays with the last wisps of an early mist floating over the great golden paddocks.

'Don't you like her, Clarry?' asked Rob, patting the neck of the pretty grey pony he held on a royal-blue lead.

'She's beautiful!' Clarissa wept.

'She certainly is, compared to Cuddles,' Ian said critically, 'but why are you crying?'

'I don't know—I'm so happy!'

'Then why don't you try her, Clarry?' Rob suggested with a grin.

'All right. What's her name?'

'Dad said to tell you to choose one for her yourself. Mum will be home some time this morning, by the way.'

'I know. Um . . .' Clarissa closed her eyes tightly. 'Holly—that's what I'll call her!'

'Holly? Where did you get that from?'

'I don't know,' Clarissa said vaguely. 'But it sounds nice, doesn't it? And it goes with Kingston.'

Both boys laughed, and for ever afterwards, the pony was known as Holly Kingston.

But at two o'clock the same day Mrs Jacobs was in a flat spin and Clarissa's mother was looking mystified.

'But why should she go off like this?' she demanded

of her housekeeper and her son. 'After going to all the trouble of organising this party for her—I don't understand it!'

'She's probably scared stiff, Mum,' said Ian, and glanced at Mrs Jacobs for confirmation.

'That could be it, Mrs Kingston,' Mrs Jacobs agreed. 'She doesn't know any kids of her own age.'

Clarissa's mother made an impatient sound. 'Anyway we've got to find her. Mrs Jacobs, remind me to take this up with her governess when the new term starts. I must say I hadn't thought of it—she seems so happy!'

'She is,' Ian muttered darkly, and went off to organise a search party.

It was Rob who found her, in a dim corner of the old, disused shearing shed, with tear streaks on her face, her long fair hair tangled and minus one blue bow and her white voile party dress with its blue sash that had arrived with her mother that morning, sporting some dusty marks.

He was silent for a moment or two with an odd little smile twisting his lips as he made out her dejected figure in the half gloom of the shed because the windows had been boarded up years ago, thinking that it was the first time he'd seen her in a dress since she was about three.

'Clarry,' he said then, 'what's this?'

'Oh, Rob!' Clarissa jumped up and cast herself into his arms. 'I don't want to go to the party. Please don't tell them you found me!'

'But it's your own party . . .'

'I hate parties!'

'Have you ever been to one?'

'No, but . . .'

'Listen, there's nothing to be scared of. They're only

other little girls and you'll play games and have a lovely tea and lots of presents . . . What's wrong with that?'

'I don't know any of them!'

Rob Randall frowned down at her and seemed about to say something, then visibly changed his mind and said instead, 'All the same, I bet you'll enjoy it.'

'Did you enjoy your birthday parties?' she asked him.

He laughed. 'I didn't have any, actually. But I'm sure I would have.'

'Oh.' Clarissa considered this. 'Is seventeen too old to start having birthday parties?' she asked.

'Much too old,' he said with a grin which he smothered immediately. 'Now listen,' he went on gravely, 'everyone's worried sick about you and you've got yourself into a bit of a mess again . . .' He put her on her feet and turned her around resignedly. 'Anything torn?'

Clarissa screwed her head round at an impossible angle to try to look down her back. 'Don't think so.'

'Then we'll have to hope Mrs Jacobs can do a rush job on you. Coming?' He held out a hand.

Clarissa slipped hers into it, but hung back. 'I don't know what to say to . . . them,' she said tremulously.

Although he was only seventeen, Rob was six foot tall and Clarissa barely came up to his waist. But his face softened as he saw the fear and uncertainty in her blue-grey eyes.

'Why . . . why don't you tell them about Holly Kingston?' he suggested. 'Look, would you like me to bring her up to show them? I'm sure they'd all love her too. And Ian can bring Cuddles and we'll give them rides. How would that be?'

Clarissa brightened. 'Would you, Rob?'

'Yes—if you promise me one thing—you'll be a big, brave girl this afternoon?'

'I'll try,' she vowed.

'Where?' Ian asked laconically.

'The old shearing shed,' Rob replied.

'Scared stiff, I suppose?'

'Mmm. And in a mess. Mrs Jacobs nearly had a heart attack when she saw her!'

'She's a funny kid,' Ian said resignedly. 'Even though she's my sister. Not much else frightens her!'

'Lots of kids are shy. She reckons she doesn't know any of them.'

'I don't think she does, actually,' remarked Ian.

'Then where are they all from?'

'Neighbouring properties, I guess. Come to think of it, that's how I made my debut into society, on my seventh birthday, only I was really looking forward to it! I think Mum didn't stop to consider that we're not all the kind of social animal she is.'

'Perhaps it will only take practice for Clarry,' said Rob after a moment. 'By the way, Nip,' he went on, 'I've got a job for you this afternoon.' He explained.

'You're *kidding*!' shouted Ian, his fourteen-year-old voice slipping into an upper register as it still did occasionally, which annoyed him because he liked to think he was nearly grown up, and often affected a world-weary kind of cynicism which was very much in vogue at his very exclusive boarding school. 'And don't call me Nip!'

'I'm not kidding. It was the only way I could get her to feel ... happier about this damn party, and she's *your* sister, anyway!'

'Dear Ian and Robert,' Narelle Kingston said warmly,

'what would I do without you?'

She was an extremely young-looking thirty-four-year-old brunette with a fabulous figure and sense of style that carried her frequently into the society pages. She also had speaking grey eyes, and it had more than once been said of her that she could charm you out of your last cent and have you congratulate her at the same time. In fact it was also often said that Bernard and Narelle Kingston were the perfect couple—that she was the perfect foil for the rather strong, silent type of man Bernard was.

So far as looks went, Ian had inherited his mother's dark vitality, while Clarissa took after her father, whom she adored but from a distance. One of the reasons for this might have been that the Kingstons spent very little time at Mirrabilla. Another undoubtedly was that Clarissa had once heard herself described by her mother as 'my little afterthought'. Not that she'd understood what it meant at the time, but the rather wry way it had been said had alerted her imagination, always extremely vivid. The result had been an instinctive decision not to be any trouble to both her parents, for that matter.

Which could have been why Narelle Kingston got such a surprise when Clarissa had disappeared just before her party, and Bernard Kingston had taken time to ponder why Clarissa's gratitude for the pony he'd bought her had had a slightly anxious quality to it.

'Well, at least Clarry seems to be enjoying herself,' Ian remarked to his mother as the three of them stood on the front lawn and watched eight little girls tucking in with great gusto to the party fare laid out on a table.

Narelle waved a hand. 'She'll get over this shyness,' she said. 'Do you know, I feel quite exhausted. If you two hadn't arrived with the horses I was beginning to think I was staring my greatest social failure in the face! Why Robert,' she marvelled, 'how you've grown! Or have I been away for too long?'

'I'm not that far behind Rob, Mum,' Ian said.

'No, you're not, darling. But goodness me, it only seems like yesterday when you were two little nippers. How's your father, Robert?'

'Very well, thank you, Mrs Kingston.'

'I must go down and see him. What are you doing now Robert? Still at school?'

'Yes. But I finish at the end of the year.'

'And then?'

'I'm going to college.'

'Will you come back every weekend as you've done in high school?' she asked.

'Probably.'

'Until a little girl-friend arrives on the scene, no doubt,' Narelle Kingston said rather archly.

Ian Kingston glanced at his best friend and mentor—apart from school, and that because Rob had spent his high school years at an ordinary state school as a weekly boarder—they had been inseparable since he could remember. But he couldn't help wondering if Rob was going to blush at his mother's unfortunate remark as he himself still had the regrettable tendency to do at the mention of girl-friends.

Not a flicker of colour disturbed his friend's lean, suntanned cheeks, though, as he looked up briefly at Narelle Kingston out of those remarkably blue eyes. And he said equably, 'I mightn't have time for girl-friends.'

'What are you going to study?'

'Engineering and mining. But part-time.'

'Well! I must speak to Mr Kingston about this. He

might be able to get you a job.'

'I already have the offer of one in a draughting office, thank you, Mrs Kingston,' Rob said politely.

Narelle widened her beautiful grey eyes. 'You don't waste any time, do you?'

'It's only two months until the end of the year,' he pointed out.

'Rob's going to top the state, I expect,' said Ian.

'Your father will be proud of you! So will we all— oops! I didn't think little girls fought!'

Two little girls were certainly fighting over a party favour, however, and it took both Narelle and Mrs Jacobs to sort it out.

And one little girl, namely Clarissa Kingston, was very sick that night.

'I knew she'd enjoy herself—she must have, to have eaten enough to make her sick!' her mother said.

In fact, Clarissa had not eaten nearly enough to make her sick. It was pure reaction to an afternoon of almost intolerable strain that had done it. An afternoon she'd only got through by constantly reminding herself that she had promised Rob to be a big brave girl—a promise in essence that she was going to make to him quite often in the next years, as it turned out.

The next crisis in Clarissa's young life came when she was ten.

The preceding three years had been happy and contented for the most part, although, despite her governess's best efforts on her mother's instructions, she hadn't conquered her shyness. But her life at Mirrabilla had more than compensated for that, although she had taken to worrying about her father. Had she been older, she would have understood the burdens he carried, perhaps, and known that they were not only of a financial nature. And known what only a few people suspected, that Bernard and Narelle Kingston were not so ideally suited. That her father was a man rather torn between his love for Mirrabilla and the fascination of a dazzling woman who was his wife but didn't share his longing for a quiet, country-orientated life. Narelle Kingston rarely enjoyed Mirrabilla unless she was entertaining there.

But Clarissa had made a good friend of Rob's quiet father, although it puzzled her that they should be two such different kinds of people, the Randalls, junior and senior. For Rob's father was obviously quite content to devote his life to breeding sheep, although he could talk knowledgeably about most subjects under the sun.

She had asked him about it once, putting her thoughts into words haltingly and in a rather roundabout manner.

'Do you think if he had his *own* place, Rob would be like you, Mr Randall?' she asked, glancing around the comfortable cottage Rob and his father shared.

'Like me? No, Clarry.'

'I mean I know he should qualify at something, but I sometimes think . . . he won't ever stop.'

Peter Randall grimaced as he thought of his only son who had topped the state in his Senior Certificate, who had almost been born, it sometimes seemed to him, doing things better than his peers, and so many different kinds of things. He could ride better than anyone on Mirrabilla, drove, shear faster if he set his mind to it. And yet where he will find his ultimate satisfaction is something that also worries me, he mused, and glanced at Clarissa.

He sucked his old pipe. 'Something of an enigma,'

he mused. 'I think,' he went on slowly, 'he's inherited some sort of driving force, Clarry.'

'From his mother?' Clarissa knew Rob's mother had died when he was very young.

Peter Randall smiled. 'No. I once made a very difficult decision, Clarry, regarding Rob. I won't bore you with the details, but while I'm not sorry I made it, there is someone I would like Rob to know and make his own judgement about, and not, for that matter, feel bound by any judgements *I* made now that he's been brought up the way I saw fit. Because he and this person are very much alike and nothing can change that . . . I don't suppose I'm making the least bit of sense to you, which is a pity, Clarry,' he added meditatively, 'because I think you understand Rob rather well, if not better than most.'

Clarissa said nothing, because she had been puzzling the first part of this speech and wondering if this someone was a relative—it had to be, but who she had no idea. Rob and Peter Randall didn't seem to have any. As to how well she understood Rob, how could she tell even his father that she loved and trusted Rob as a special friend? Ian, for example, still teased her mercilessly upon occasion, having overheard her asking Rob to marry her—a proposal spoken in perfect innocence before her seventh birthday, but a cause for more and more embarrassment to her as she grew older.

But she did say finally, 'I . . . oh!' The clock on the wall caught her eyes. 'I'm late for lessons. 'Bye, Mr Randall!'

And she flew up the track towards the house with her long fair plaits flying and feeling a certain sense of relief.

Her other cause not so much for worry but regret during those years was that she saw less of Rob. Because he was doing his degree part-time and working, he didn't get the advantage of the long vacations, but he did often hitch a ride home at weekends, and if Ian was home, it was almost like old times. But Rob did come home every long Christmas holiday, and was paid to help his father out and also to lend a hand up at the homestead, mostly acting as barman at the endless house-parties Narelle seemed to give over the festive season. He was even presented with his own black dinner suit for the grander occasions.

'Doesn't Rob look nice?' Clarissa had said shyly to her mother, the first time she had seen him dressed in it.

Narelle hadn't answered immediately, and Clarissa had glanced up enquiringly to see that she was staring thoughtfully at Rob.

'Mum?'

'Mmm? Oh yes, he does. I might have to keep an eye out for our younger, more impressionable lady guests,' Narelle said then, with a twinkle in her eye. 'Well, seen enough, poppet? I think it's time for bed.'

'All right. You look super too, Mum. Better than anyone else.'

'Thank you darling!' And she *had* looked superb, in a figure-hugging strapless dress in a shimmering watermark taffeta that matched her eyes.

Then Ian had come up with their father and Clarissa had felt rather like the odd man out. Ian was allowed to attend these parties now, but not only that—he and Bernard Kingston seemed to have grown very close together lately. Not that Clarissa had resented this—she was happy for Ian and her father.

She just wished she was old enough to be included.

Then the blow fell.

It was not so much that she hadn't known about it for several months, but that she'd pushed it to the back of her mind, hoping it would mysteriously go away. But there came a day in late January when reality was only an afternoon and a night away. And it seemed only natural that the only person she could confide in was Rob, although she'd vowed not to. But he found her crying quietly and quite hopelessly into Holly Kingston's neck.

She didn't know it, but he'd come into the stables silently and watched her for a minute or two. Then he walked over to her and lifted up one fair plait.

'Clarry? What's wrong?'

She tensed convulsively and lifted her tear-streaked face. 'N-nothing!'

He smiled slightly. 'It must be something, but I think I can guess anyway. Boarding school?'

Clarissa looked away and wiped her nose on the back of her hand.

'Do you know,' he said slowly, 'there's one thing to be said for being away from home. It makes it even more special to come back to.'

'But it couldn't *be* more special to me than it is now,' she said huskily. 'I don't want to go away. And,' her next words echoed an old torment, 'I won't know anyone!'

'Clarry, come and sit over here with me.' He led her towards some lucerne bales and they sat down side by side. 'Do you know something else? A whole lot of people feel like you do.'

'Scared, you mean?' she whispered.

'Shy and scared. In fact most of the kids at your new school, the new ones, will be feeling nervous and worried, just as most of them will be nice kids and wanting to make friends.'

Clarissa was silent.

'The other thing is,' he said after a while, 'being very shy is something you can't help, but it is something you can try to change, otherwise you'll be miserable often. Just remember there isn't anything to be frightened of.'

'They'll all laugh at me,' she muttered.

Unseen, Rob looked upwards for heavenly assistance. 'Try thinking of Holly Kingston,' he suggested.

'Th-that's another thing,' she blurted. 'She'll forget me.'

'She will not,' he said positively, but put an arm around her shaking shoulders. 'Dad will think of something to keep her occupied,' he assured her. 'Anyway, it's only going to be a couple of months at a time. And if you really feel . . . down, sometimes, you could think of how proud we all would be to know you're coping and really trying to make a go of it.'

Clarissa lifted her head. 'Would you be proud of me, Rob?' she asked tremulously.

'Would I ever!'

'Oh, Rob,' a glowing smile lit her thin, dirty little face. 'I'll try, then, I promise!' And she hid her face in his shoulder for a moment, and he hugged her. 'I'm awfully proud of you,' she said then. 'For doing so well in your exams. Soon you'll be an engineer, won't you?'

'Still a couple of years to go, Clarry,' he said wryly, and didn't know how happy the thought of this made her. 'Tell you what, seeing that you're going away tomorrow and I am the day after, should we go for a ride?'

'Oh yes, please!'

For months afterwards, Clarissa could remember

every detail of that ride. The smell of heat and dust in
the paddocks, the creaking of their saddles, the way
Rob handled the frisky chestnut gelding he was riding
that took about one stride to Holly Kingston's four . . .
The creek they stopped at to have a drink and rest the
horses and the slow amble home through the paddocks
as the sun set . . .

The next morning she sat upright in the back of the
car beside her mother, dressed up in her new school
clothes and waved bravely to the unusually large
number of people who seemed to have gathered.

'At least she's not crying,' said Ian.

'No,' Mrs Jacobs agreed, and wiped away a tear of
her own on her apron.

'Well, all kids like us have to go through this,' Ian
offered. 'I don't remember creating such a stir when I
first went to boarding school!'

No one replied, and Ian suddenly realised that the
reason for his vague feeling of moodiness was actually
caused by a feeling of concern for his young sister. 'She
just looks so . . . little,' he explained, which caused Mrs
Jacobs to take a deep steadying breath that failed her
so she turned away precipitously and ran back into the
house.

'Now what I have said?' he enquired irritably of
Rob, who had stood quite silent since Clarissa had
said goodbye, her face pale with the strain of
composure.

'You hit the nail on the head,' he said, 'that's all.
Small and vulnerable.'

'But she's got to learn, hasn't she, Rob?'

'Yes. This seems a bit like throwing her in at the
deep end, though. Couldn't she have gone to a day
school in Sydney first?'

Ian was silent. Then he said cryptically, 'That might

have cramped Mum's style a bit. I mean,' he added hastily, 'she's not home a lot, what with dinners and balls and lunches and the races—Clarry could have been as lonely at home, lonelier.'

Rob shrugged. 'I guess so.' He turned away.

'Hey, Rob, I've been meaning to ask you something!' Ian brightened. 'What are you doing over the Easter break?'

'Nothing that I know of.'

'Come down and spend it with me.'

'I . . .' Rob hesitated.

'Now if you're going to start all that nonsense, forget it,' said Ian forcefully. 'You're not only an employee, you're part of the family. Anyway, you deserve a break in the big smoke, surely! You've worked like a slave for years. Besides which, I'm giving a party, a formal party, and I promise you,' he said slyly, 'there'll be some gorgeous chicks there.' Ian had quite lost his initial embarrassment over the matter of girls.

Rob Randall regarded his friend amusedly. 'Why are you giving a party?'

'For my eighteenth birthday. What's wrong with that? Just because you're twenty now . . .'

'Nothing wrong with it,' Rob admitted.

'Then come! I've got lots of friends now, I'd like you to meet. We could also,' added Ian as if struck by a sudden thought, 'take Clarry out somewhere.'

That outing was to cause Clarissa immeasurable joy, only when she thought about it afterwards, which she did often, it was to feel some confusion and a lot of pain.

Confusion because Rob had been different. Not towards her, but she'd detected an inner tension that she couldn't account for. She had wondered if he'd felt out of place in the big Sydney house on the Harbour, but he hadn't *seemed* at all out of place. Confusion too, because it had slowly begun to dawn on her that her parents weren't getting along as they always had, and *they'd* been at unspoken loggerheads—or so it had seemed to Clarissa.

But really, for years her confusion had been swamped by grief and pain. For Easter Monday was the last day she had seen her brother Ian alive.

And anyway, the rift between her parents was well and truly in the open after Ian's death, as a conversation Clarissa overhead one night demonstrated. Not that she understood the undercurrents, but the bitterness was impossible to miss.

'. . . *I* didn't agree to flying lessons for Ian, Bernard! You didn't even consult me!'

'Why should I have—actually, I did.' Clarissa's father's voice was raw and rasping. 'You said—oh! "Should I wear this green and blue . . ." something or other?'

'For heaven's sake! I probably didn't even hear you.'

'Do you ever, Narelle?'

'*Yes*. Too often.'

'What's that supposed to mean?'

There was silence, then Narelle said, 'Bernard, I can't believe he's dead . . .'

'*You* can't.'

'He was so young.'

'I'm glad you noticed. Has it occurred to you that Clarissa's suffering?'

'I . . . I suppose so,' she admitted.

'You *suppose* so?'

'She'll get over it . . .'

At that point Clarissa had crept away.

Ian had been buried at Mirrabilla and whenever Clarissa was home from school she kept fresh flowers on his grave in the small family cemetery. Sometimes they were only little posies of wildflowers, but Rob, who always visited Ian's grave too, when he came home, said it didn't matter—that Ian would probably have preferred them anyway because they'd been picked from the places he'd known so well. Rob had suffered very much too, Clarissa knew, because sometimes he stopped and lifted his head just as if he was expecting Ian to come flying down the stable path.

She was nearly thirteen when Rob qualified as a mining engineer, an old hand at boarding school but for all that one of the quietest girls in her class, and she still cried into her pillow on the first night back each term. But she had discovered an inner sense of fortitude and did have some friends.

'It's not so bad now, is it, Clarry?' Rob had said to her once.

'No,' she had answered honestly.

But being nearly thirteen had posed some more problems for her, and not only the one associated with Rob qualifying and going away. Problems of puberty and a maturing body which embarrassed her somewhat ...

'Well, well, Clarry,' Mrs Jacobs said, 'who would have thought it, but you're going to have a lovely little figure in a few years' time.'

'You mean I'm going to keep on ... growing like this?'

Mrs Jacobs laughed. 'Don't look so horrified! I'd say you're going to end up just right for your height. In the meantime, I don't think I can let these school dresses down any more, and you need some new bras. I'll speak to your mum. Provided I can catch up with her,' she muttered beneath her breath.

And that had been the essence of another problem for Clarissa. For not only was there an ever-widening gulf between her parents, but they seemed to be growing further and further away from her. It occurred to Clarissa that her father had never got over Ian's death and might never do so. If it had to be either of us, perhaps it should have been me, she'd thought once with a shiver.

In fact Rob's qualifying proved the least of her problems, for he got a job in a South Coast colliery and until the unbelievable happened, when she was fifteen, the status quo was more or less retained, because he often spent weekends with his father.

By the time she had turned fifteen, she had got more used to this new Clarissa Kingston who now had a clearly defined waist, slender rounded hips, long legs and a bust. Not that anyone else seemed to notice it. Certainly her own circle of men treated her not one whit differently. Although she did begin to understand dimly that they had gradually tightened their highly effective, protective circle about her, so that there was never any doubt on Mirrabilla that the boss's daughter was off-limits. It was an invisible thing, though, for the most part, except perhaps at times like shearing-time, when there were strangers on the property. But then Mrs Jacobs was equally on guard in this matter.

So it confused Clarissa a lot to find that she was beginning to think differently of Rob. And to find herself wondering about his girl-friends, which she thought he must have, although he never brought any home to Mirrabilla. And to wonder sometimes, with great daring, what it would be like to be kissed by him.

For even in a greatly liberated age where these matters were much discussed at school, and magazines smuggled in that explained so many mysteries in almost horrifying detail, she could somehow never progress beyond the stage of being kissed. And even that left her feeling guilty and breathless. Guilty, because she couldn't help feeling she was undermining her very special relationship with Rob.

Naturally she went out of her way to prevent this becoming common knowledge—and least of all known to him.

Then the blow fell. Peter Randall died after the briefest illness, leaving Bernard Kingston in possession of his will and two letters.

'I don't believe it!' Narelle Kingston exclaimed in tones of shock. 'Why was he so secretive? Rob's father?'

'He said—in his letter to Rob—that he and his father had come to hate each other, that they were totally different people and that his father had not been able to come to terms with the fact that his only son was not interested in making money, had little use for it—even deplored people who pursued it. He also said, and I think this has hurt and bewildered Rob, that he could see a lot of his grandfather in him. I tried to explain to Rob that he might have meant the fascination for mining that was in his blood. That was how Robert T. Randall started his fortune, in silver, lead and tin mining. It's still the backbone of Randall's Inc.,' Bernard said.

'What are you going to do?'

'I have no choice but to contact Robert T. Randall as requested in the will, Narelle.'

'My God, if only I'd known!'

'Rob?'

Clarissa peered through the gloom of the old shearing shed.

Rob Randall looked up and stared at her bleakly. Then a wry smile twisted his lips and he made way for her to sit next to him on an upturned crate.

'This takes me back,' he told her, 'to your seventh birthday.'

'I wish I could help you, the way you helped me then,' she said with difficulty.

He sighed and put an arm around her shoulders. 'But you do, Clarry, you do. I just wish I could take you with me.'

Clarissa closed her eyes and if she hadn't been so sad, she could almost have died of joy. 'Then ... you're going to your grandfather?' she said tremulously.

'Yes.'

'But you don't feel right about it?'

'I . . .' Rob hesitated. 'I can't help feeling I'm being disloyal to my father.'

'What's he like?' she asked.

'He's very old with a lot of white hair and a very arrogant manner, Clarry. But he ... well, he broke down and cried, and he said there were some things he could never forgive himself for. He also said—and this is really ironic—that if I wanted to follow in my father's footsteps and breed sheep for the rest of my life, I had his blessing. Then he asked me ... what I'd done with my life so far, and we discussed it and—we're two of a kind, it seems, in that respect.'

'I think your father always knew that,' she said, recalling a conversation she'd had years ago with Peter Randall and suddenly understanding it. 'I don't think he minded.'

'How do you know?'

She told him.

'Did he actually say that?'

'Yes. I didn't know what he meant at the time, but now it makes sense.'

Rob was silent for a long time. Then he pulled her close and said huskily, 'Thanks—I guess that evens the score. Actually it far outweighs anything I did for you on your seventh birthday.'

'It wasn't only then. Will you come and see me sometimes, Rob?'

He held her away from him and something in those very blue eyes sharpened briefly. Then he said, 'I'll never forget you, Clarry.'

'I'll be grown up soon, Rob,' Clarissa heard herself say quite out of the blue, and she blushed with horror.

He smiled down at her, but his eyes remained serious as he said, 'Not too soon, I hope.'

'Why?'

'Because these things take time. You don't have to rush it. And anyway, we'll always be friends.'

The fire Rob had built up was still casting flickering shadows on the bedroom walls as Clarissa came out of her reverie briefly with a sigh.

And that was Rob's way of telling me it was no good cherishing any romantic notions of him, she thought. And that was why he stayed away—one of the reasons. The trouble was, it didn't change the way I felt at all.

But what I'll *never* understand is how I could have reached eighteen and not really known the trouble Mirrabilla was in . . .

CHAPTER THREE

'I DON'T care!' Narelle Kingston said stubbornly. 'You're turning eighteen, you're a Kingston and this will be your coming-out party.'

'Mum, I honestly think we should forget it,' Clarissa said desperately. She had barely recovered from the death of her father and the last thing she wanted was a coming-out party. 'It just doesn't seem right! I loved Daddy even if you didn't,' she added, and turned away abruptly.

If there had been anyone she could have confided in about the increasingly savage nature of her parents' relationship before Bernard Kingston's death of a heart attack, it might have been Rob. But it was so long since she'd seen him, she knew he had forgotten about her. Although he had come to her father's funeral. But she had been so consumed by grief for a man she hadn't really known that well, she had been hardly able to talk at all. Only to feel instinctively that one by one the mainstays of her life were disappearing, and to feel so much regret that she hadn't had the chance to get to know her father better.

'Clarissa,' Narelle said with a suddenly steely look in her grey eyes, 'before you pass judgement on me, my dear, go out and find yourself a man with impossible expectations and try to live up to them.'

Clarissa turned back, her blue-grey eyes suddenly blazing, and her mother had flinched and all of a sudden looked a little old. 'Darling, I didn't mean that,' she said rather tremulously. 'He was a better

48

man than I am, Gunga Din ... God knows. But he would have liked to see you ... well, you're the last Kingston, Clarissa. It's been a proud name. He would have wanted this for you, I know. Did they teach you to dance at school? They certainly charged enough in fees! I must think about a dress.'

The dress was exquisite, but it was much more than that. It altered Clarissa's image both subtly and quite dramatically.

'Well,' said Mrs Jacobs eyeing Clarissa critically on the night of the party, 'I hope she knows what she's doing.'

Clarissa looked perplexed. 'What do you mean?'

'Nothing,' Mrs Jacobs said vaguely. 'Hair up too!'

Clarissa regarded Mrs Jacobs steadily and fondly. For here was one mainstay at least that showed no sign of disappearing. She now knew something of Mrs Jacobs' history, enough to understand her almost Victorian outlook on life. For Mrs Jacobs had been born on a sheep station, married without ever leaving that property, widowed within a few short years and, to cut a short story even shorter, had never been exposed to city or any other kind of broader life. Which was not to say that she wasn't a jewel amongst housekeepers or didn't know the finer points of life when it came to cuisine—or, for that matter, a whole host of other things.

She had always insisted, for example, that Clarissa go out and about on the station wearing long sleeves and trousers in the fiercest heat. 'Got to look after your skin,' she'd said. 'You don't want to be dried up like a prune before you're sixteen. And keep your hat on.' She had even gone further. She had insisted that pure lanolin—and Mirrabilla was a better place than most to come by that—was wonderful for complexions, to which Clarissa certainly appeared to bear mute testimony. But it was odd, Clarissa had often thought, that lanolin was about the only part, except perhaps for its wool, of a sheep that Mrs Jacobs could bear. She certainly never ate mutton or lamb or served it.

She also believed that young girls should be trained in all the housewifely arts, and had so trained Clarissa. 'Never know when it might come in handy,' she'd said frequently. 'You can rely on a man being charmed by other things only up to a point.'

But otherwise, on the subject of men, she had never had much to say.

Yet on the night of Clarisa's eighteenth birthday party, it was a subject she did have on her mind, although Clarissa didn't know it—only that something was bothering Mrs Jacobs.

'My hair looks nice, though, don't you think, Mrs Jacobs?' she said.

Mrs Jacobs' face softened and she patted Clarissa's cheek and agreed with her, then left her, making some excuse about checking up on the hired help. But as she wandered around the old homestead, it was obvious that Mrs Jacobs was worried. And not about the state of the house she had prepared so carefully for this party. In fact she stood in front of one of the many beautiful flower arrangements for at least two minutes, and didn't even notice that some water from the vase had spilled on to the the beautiful Chinese rosewood table it stood on—something that would never have escaped her attention otherwise.

But finally she roused herself and walked away muttering, 'Man bait, that's what it is . . .'

It could have been said that Clarissa's dress was just that. Only it was much more subtle, which was probably why she herself didn't realise what the beautiful white dress was all about. The colour, for one thing, seemed suitable for an eighteen-year-old, although she had been vaguely surprised her mother hadn't chosen blue, which was what Clarissa wore a lot of, especially a certain misty blue that did great things for her eyes. She didn't know that in choosing white, her mother was proclaiming her virginal status for all the world to see.

Then there was the style, a strapless heart-shaped bodice that clung to her figure, as did the rest of the dress to below her knees where it frothed out. But the bodice was discreetly covered by a filmy little cape that buttoned at the neck and skimmed her shoulders, and parted tantalisingly at the front when she moved.

It was this mixture of restraint and a superb cut and fit of the rose-patterned taffeta and tulle dress that proclaimed something else for the world to see! That there was a lovely slender and curved body with high tender little breasts and long legs beneath the rich material. And with her hair piled on top of her head and threaded with little white flowers, not much make-up and only a faint glossy colour on her young lips, Clarissa looked quite bewitchingly desirable.

She created a sensation, just as Mrs Jacobs had known she would, and feared. Mrs Jacobs had more than an inkling of the true state of affairs on Mirrabilla and a certain cynicism towards Marelle Kingston. But when she saw how every man present eyed Clarissa discreetly and not so discreetly, many of them old enough to be her father, her blood began to boil and she thought, no . . . she wouldn't! Would she . . .?

As usual, the party in itself was rather an ordeal for

Clarissa, and although she didn't know it as she stood by her mother's side, her inner nerves communicated themselves externally in a way that added to her attraction so that she looked regal and poised and cool when in fact it was the chill of her old enemy, shyness.

Then, after dinner, she caught sight of a dark head amongst the throng, and turned to her mother to say in stunned accents, 'You didn't tell me you'd invited Rob!'

'Didn't I? Must have slipped my mind. Anyway, I thought he wasn't coming—he's left it rather late. Where is he?'

'O-over there,' Clarissa stammered.

'Then we should go and greet him,' Narelle said serenely, and shepherded Clarissa through the crowd until they stood behind Robert Randall, who turned slowly.

There was a moment's dead silence.

Clarissa stared up at him with her heart in her eyes for an instant, thinking dazedly, it's been *three* years—how could you?

But almost immediately her thick lashes veiled her eyes as her mind reeled with shock. Because it was as if someone else was standing before her. Not her Rob, but a man she didn't know. A man who was commanding the attention of most of the people in the room, respectful glances from the men, admiring glances from the women—a tall, dark stranger, a man of the world, very obviously, a man of power and with something in the lines and angles of his face which suggested that power had brought him some disillusionment.

Then her mother was saying, 'Why, Rob! I'm so glad you were able to come. I have to tell you we've really missed you. Mirrabilla hasn't been the same without you, has it, Clarissa?'

Robert Randall said automatically, 'Hello, Mrs Kingston.' Then, 'Happy birthday, Clarry.'

'It's not my birthday today,' she murmured foolishly.

'I know that. It was two days ago, but . . .'

Clarissa's lashes flew up, but to her consternation the band struck up for the first dance of the evening and her mother said, 'I think it would be quite fitting for you to dance this first dance with Clarissa, Rob. On behalf of her . . . father.'

A curious thing happened—or so Clarissa thought. Rob turned his head slightly to look at her mother, a look that her mother returned boldly, and for some reason the air crackled with tension. Until he said, 'It would be a pleasure.'

They danced in silence—not only because they were the focus of attention, the only couple on the floor, but because Clarissa's heart seemed to be thumping in her breast quite unnaturally. Then the tempo changed and the spotlight went out to a round of applause and other couples streamed on to the floor.

Only then did Rob break the silence. 'You've grown, Clarry. Taller.'

'It could be my hair,' she shrugged.

'What's wrong?' he asked.

'Nothing!'

'Come outside on to the verandah with me for a moment, then,' he said, releasing her body but keeping hold of her hand.

She hesitated, then followed him out to stand a little awkwardly in a pool of light.

'You look very lovely,' he told her.

'Th-thank you.'

'But also a little hurt and reproachful. I can

understand why.'

'Oh no,' she said hastily. 'No, I'm not!' But she thought her voice betrayed her and hoped desperately that he hadn't noticed the slight quiver in it. 'I . . . I'm sorry about your grandfather. You didn't have very long with him.'

'No. I'm sorry about your father—I didn't really get a chance at the funeral. It must have come as an awful shock.'

Clarissa averted her eyes. 'It did. But he was very unhappy, so . . . I mean, I don't think he ever got over Ian.'

'He had you,' Rob pointed out.

'Well, yes . . .' She bit her lip and looked up at him, thinking fleetingly, but it wasn't what he really wanted, like you . . . And she blushed suddenly as she remembered wondering what it would be like to be kissed by Rob.

He observed all this in silence, and she got the horrible feeling he could see into her mind and she was about to turn away when he dug a hand into his pocket and pulled out a flat velvet box, saying abruptly, 'I brought you a present. I hope it's not too young for you.'

It was a silver charm bracelet and each charm was an exquisitely worked miniature horse—a racehorse complete with tiny jockey, a drover on horseback with a sheepdog at foot, a dancing stallion, a gypsy horse with a hat on, and even one that looked just like Holly Kingston.

'Oh!' breathed Clarissa, turning the charms over in her fingers. 'Oh no! Why should it be too young for me? Where did you get all these horses?'

'I had it specially made,' Rob said rather sombrely, his blue eyes resting fleetingly on the shadow between her breasts that the heart-shaped bodice revealed and the filmy cape was not, at that moment, covering. 'Then you're still mad about horses?' he asked, his gaze coming back to rest on her face.

'Oh. I see what you mean,' she said, looking up ruefully. 'But I think I might always be that.'

He said, 'I'm glad.'

'I'd like to wear it now. I . . .'

'Here, let me put it on. I don't know if it goes with your finery. Diamonds or pearls might have been a better choice.'

'I don't care. It's the nicest present I've had since Holly Kingston herself. She's had two foals, you know. No, you don't, of course—how silly of me!'

'Clarry,' said Rob compellingly, his fingers still about her wrist, and she looked up again. 'I'm *sorry*. I thought it was for the best.'

Clarissa went quite still and stared into his eyes. Then she drew herself up with unconscious dignity. 'Oh, it was,' she said very quietly. 'I understand that. All the same, thank you for this. I . . . think I ought to be going in now.'

'Why, there you are, Clarissa,' said Narelle, coming up to them quite silently. 'I wondered what had become of you. It is your party, darling,' she said gaily, 'so make the best of it! And in the meantime I'll take care of Rob.'

In fact, Rob didn't stay very long after that, and Clarissa didn't know whether to be relieved or sad, which she was anyway. Nor was her state of mind helped by the fact that her mother told her afterwards that they would be moving to Sydney for the next few months, that her debut into society had only just begun. Clarissa also detected an unusual air about her mother which bothered her slightly and was hard to explain, beyond saying that it was like a flash of her mother's old brilliance which had, she suddenly realised, been a little doused lately.

She went to sleep that night with the charm bracelet under her pillow and tears on her cheeks.

The ensuing months assumed nightmare proportions for Clarissa. True to her word, her mother exposed her to society on every possible occasion, and dressed her superbly. But by this time Clarissa *had* begun to be aware that all was not well. She overheard guarded telephone conversations her mother had with accountants and solicitors, by the sound of it. She worried about what was happening to Mirrabilla with no one at the helm, so to speak. She asked her mother about these things, only to be told not to worry her pretty head about it. And in the meantime, she went to parties and balls and luncheons and the races, and worried about that too. She was not, she knew, the kind of social animal her mother was, as Ian might have said, but this 'season' seemed to be her mother's dearest wish for her, so she tried—she really tried.

She saw very little of Rob which again made her sad and glad. And not only because on the odd occasions their paths did cross, he was always with some beautiful, sophisticated woman but also because she was so uneasy and uncomfortable within, however hard she tried at being a budding young socialite, although she had assumed a veneer of sophistication herself to cope with it all, especially the attention she received from men.

It was odd how few people realised that her sociability was barely skin deep.

It was unfortunate, as it turned out, that Robert

Randall should have been on hand when it deserted her.

The occasion was a charity ball. Clarissa went with a party and she wore an off-the-shoulder gown in a colour that resembled pale, orangey moonlight. Her mother was to have gone, being one of the organisers, but had developed a streaming head cold.

Amongst Clarissa's party was James Halliday, wealthy, quite a lot older than her, amusing although sometimes rather disturbingly cynical, and unattached. He was also very much interested in Clarissa.

She had noticed this and contrived to keep him at arm's length—something which made him more and more interested. On the whole, however, he had played his hand quite cleverly, but it had never once dawned on him that Clarissa was unaware of the strength of the attraction she held for him.

So that, on the night of the ball, when she seemed to be more maddeningly cool than ever, he quite uncharacteristically lost his head. He thought her extra coolness was all part of the ploy and, with some wryness, that it was succeeding.

He didn't know that Clarissa in fact thought she was being quite nice to him. She had danced with him and tried to concentrate her thoughts on his amusing conversstion. She even, now, allowed him to dance her outside on to the ballroom balcony. She even smiled up at him, then turned away to study the moonlight over the Harbour, and to wonder who the new woman with Rob was. He hadn't introduced her when they'd met briefly, but Clarissa had noticed almost everything about her which, put into a nutshell, read—striking, intelligent-looking and very sophisticated.

It was while she was thinking these thoughts, standing in the moonlight in her dress that was nearly the same colour, that James Halliday lost his head.

'All right,' he drawled, puting a hand on her bare shoulder and turning her towards him, 'if it's marriage you're after, you've got it. As soon as you like. But in the meantime, this . . .'

He actually surprised himself considerably with these words, which was why he might not have noticed the look of stunned shock in Clarissa's eyes as he drew her into his arms and began to kiss her passionately.

She didn't resist for a moment, then she wrenched her mouth away, protesting, 'No . . . you don't understand!'

But James Halliday at that moment understood several things. That her cool young lips drove him mad, that the feel of her slender body in his arms confirmed what he had already known—to be the master of it promised incredible delights, that for once her mother wasn't hovering in attendance . . . that if the price tag for Clarissa included Mirrabilla, as it was rumoured, he would pay up gladly.

So it came as a most unpleasant shock to him, after he had overpowered Clarissa completely, torn her dress and rendered her numb with terror and breathless and bruised, to feel an iron hand on *his* shoulder, and to hear someone commanding him to let her go in such disgusted freezing accents that he did.

It came as a worse shock to find himself staring into Robert Randall's cold, very blue eyes.

But to crown it all, Clarissa stumbled into her rescuer's arms as if it was the most natural thing in the world to do.

All of which dealt his ego a massive blow, and it took him a few dazed moments before he could come up with a way to set that to rights.

'Well, well,' he said slowly, then, his thoughts skimming the rumours associated with Clarissa, 'what have we here? Sir Galahad? Or a higher bidder? But that's *strange*, isn't it? Doesn't make sense. I should have thought her mother would have handed . . .' But he didn't finish what he was saying, because a look of such menace entered those blue eyes, he suddenly thought better of it and turning on his heel made a rather swift exit.

'Oh, Rob!' wept Clarissa, only vaguely aware of what had been said in her distress and finding it incomprehensible anyway. 'I had no idea . . . he asked me to marry him—I think. Then he,' she swallowed, 'kissed me, and he wouldn't *listen* or stop . . .'

'You shouldn't have been out here on your own with him, Clarry,' Rob said abruptly.

'But I didn't expect . . .' Something in his tone made her lift her head, and what she saw added further cause for misery. Because it was obvious Rob was still very angry, and it had to be with her.

'I'm sorry,' she whispered, her lips trembling again and her face flushed beneath tendrils of hair which had escaped from her upswept hair-do. 'I suppose this reminds you of all the other times I've needed to be consoled. I don't seem to learn, do I?'

'This—isn't quite like those others.'

'No, worse, I guess.' She tried to smile. 'Just plain foolish this time. But I won't keep you any longer. I'll be all right now.'

He made an impatient sound. 'Do you seriously believe I'd leave you like this? Where's your mother?'

'A-at home, in bed,' Clarissa stammered. 'She's got a cold.'

'Which is precisely where you should be,' Rob said grimly.

'Oh, she didn't mind me leaving her! In fact she wanted me to come.'

He said drily, 'I can imagine. Listen, have you got everything you came with?'

'I ... only came with this.' She looked around dazedly and discovered her evening purse on the floor.

'Then stay here.' He bent down to pick it up and handed it to her. 'I'll be right back.'

'Rob ...' she began.

But he was gone. And before Clarissa had a chance to come to any other decision he was back and he took her arm in a firm grip, saying, 'Home for you, Miss Kingston, whether you like it or not.'

Clarissa sat in his car as they glided through the streets of Sydney, with her face averted and her mind in a terrible state of turmoil ... Happy as she was to have been rescued from James Halliday's clutches, why had it to be Rob? After months of—well, not *exactly* ignoring her, what unkind trick of fate had prompted him to come out on to the verandah just then? To find her in such a humiliating situation ... With the net result that she now felt like a chastened, troublesome schoolgirl. But what hurt her most was the thought that *somehow* she'd managed to get thoroughly out of step with Rob, the person she most valued and loved. How? she wondered unhappily. After that night of my eighteenth birthday, I've stayed out of his way as he seemed to want, I've not acted foolishly—I don't think. I mean, I had no idea James was ... thinking that. And all I've longed for is some sign from Rob that he understands I *know* I'm too young for him and would just like to be a friend again ...

Tears trembled on her lashes and she blinked furiously without moving her head. But they continued to fall silently.

'Clarry.'

She wouldn't look at him. 'Yes?'

'Oh hell,' Rob muttered softly, and pulled the car off the road and switched the motor off. 'Look at me, Clarry.'

She turned her head at last, and he closed his eyes briefly, then reached out a hand to brush away her tears. 'Did he hurt you?'

She said uncertainly, 'I don't think so.'

'Clarry,' he pulled a large white handkerchief out of his pocket and handed it to her, 'you told me once that your greatest ambition when you left school was to help run Mirrabilla. Have you changed your mind?'

She stared at him. 'If only you knew how much I long to be doing just that,' she said huskily.

'Then why aren't you?' he countered.

'My mother . . .' she began.

'Why don't you put your foot down, Clarry, and tell her what you want?'

'I . . . I've tried to, but . . . oh, Rob, I think Mirrabilla is in terrible trouble. And anyway, she really wants me to . . . to be doing this.'

'And you don't have the slightest idea *why* it should be so important to her, do you?' he said after a pause during which his eyes had narrowed.

Clarissa frowned. 'She's doing it for *me*. Sort of— launching me, I suppose.'

He laughed. 'She's doing that all right! Up a creek without a paddle.'

Clarissa sat in hurt, uncomprehending silence. Until Rob said, 'I didn't realise you knew about Mirrabilla's problems.'

'I don't really,' she whispered. 'Do you?'

'Not as much as I should, by the look of it,' he said

cryptically. 'Actually, after your father died I did ask her whether she needed any help in sorting things out. She refused and gave me to understand there were no problems. But lately—well, I've been hearing all sorts of rumours. Do you realise that you and she are joint shareholders in the property?'

'I don't see what difference that makes.'

'I think I — do.' And he added something beneath his breath that sounded suspiciously like, '. . . Hell and damnation!'

Which caused Clarissa to close her eyes miserably, but what he said next was so unexpected, she couldn't believe her ears.

'If it had been me tonight, Clarry, who asked you to marry me, would you have said yes?'

Her blue-grey eyes widened incredulously and her lips parted. Then she thought he must be playing some sort of an unkind joke on her and said with every scrap of youthful dignity she could muster, 'I don't think that's very funny.'

'Neither do I,' he murmured gravely but with a shadow of a smile in his eyes. 'In fact I'm deadly serious, Clarry.'

'*Rob*,' she whispered, 'you . . . you can't be. You told me—at least you made it very *clear* that I shouldn't . . . well, think of you like that.' She blushed painfully.

'Clarry, you were very young, and little girls have been known to change their minds once they've had a chance to spread their wings.'

'But . . . but,' she stammered, 'for months you've been ingoring me and . . .'

'On the contrary.'

'What do you mean?' she whispered.

Rob touched her mouth with his fingertips. 'I've been very much aware of all your doings, Clarry. I guess you could say—I've been waiting for you.'

Clarissa closed her eyes, suddenly breathless and quite speechless. But she made an effort after a minute or two. 'But I'm so different from all the — ladies I've seen you with.'

He said, 'I know. Perhaps that's what I love about you.'

'Oh, Rob!' she breathed, and started to cry again. 'I can't believe this. I thought—I really thought you didn't want to have any more to do with me, and it's made me so miserable I could have died!'

He cupped her chin in his hand and for a moment his eyes were very sombre and intent. Then, as she caught her breath, he smiled, and said, 'That's all I wanted to know.' And kissed her.

The opposition Clarissa encountered from her mother was as unexpected as it was inexplicable.

She hadn't told her that night, mainly because her mother had been sleepy and woolly-headed but also because she had wanted to hug the knowledge to herself for a bit longer.

But the next morning she stared helplessly at her mother's suddenly white face which seemed not to have anything to do with her cold, for it was much improved this morning, and said, 'Well, I've always loved him so . . .'

'Clarissa, you're not yet nineteen. How *can* you know that?'

'Because I just do.' Clarissa eyed her mother bewilderedly. 'Anyway, you were only saying the other day that you approved of early marriages.'

'*Some* . . . oh God!'

'Oh, Mum. I wish you could be happy for me. Don't you like Rob?'

Narelle sat down shakily. 'How long has this been going on for?' she asked abruptly.

'Since I was six, probably . . .'

'No, I mean have you been seeing him behind my back?'

'No.'

'Then I don't understand!'

'He said he's been waiting for me,' Clarissa told her.

Narell stared at her. Then she started to laugh, but it was a somehow chilling sound. And finally she said, 'Oh, *hell*!'

'Mum . . .?' queried Clarissa.

'Clarissa, do me a favour. Just leave me alone for a little while.'

Clarissa Kingston became Clarissa Randall in a private, morning ceremony which her mother attended, giving no sign at all that she had ever opposed the marriage. In fact, after her first confusing reaction, she had shown a change of heart that had been equally bewildering, and had been absolutely charming to Rob. She had even given in to Clarissa's wish for a very quiet wedding.

They were married one week before Clarissa's nineteenth birthday, and spent their honeymoon in Western Samoa, a beautiful South Pacific island with an age-old Polynesian culture. They flew direct, and on the thirty-odd-kilometre drive from Faleolo Airport to Aggie Grey's famous hotel, Clarissa was immediately enchanted. The scenery was breathtaking, and they passed native huts with beehive roofs, churches and the locals bathing in fresh pools.

'I thought you'd like it,' said Rob, eyeing her shining face. 'No hustle and bustle, charming people—tranquillity personified.'

Clarissa closed her eyes and sniffed luxuriously. 'It even smells beautiful and peaceful. And I feel as if I've stepped right into *Tales of the South Pacific* or that I might bump into Robert Louis Stevenson or Somerset Maugham!'

He laughed. 'You've obviously done your homework!'

But that evening, after they'd dined and were strolling in the moonlight, it occurred to Clarissa that one area of her homework, if it could be called that, had been neglected. Because all of a sudden she found herself feeling astonishingly nervous. And for the simple reason that she still hadn't got past the point of imagining herself being kissed and held, although she enjoyed both of these things very much. Especially the way Rob did it—very gently and with not the slightest sign of that bruising, impassioned fervour James Halliday had employed.

All the same, her stream of enthusiastic chatter dried up at the thought of what lay ahead.

'Clarry,' queried Rob after a while, 'what's wrong?'

'Nothing!' she protested, but she saw his teeth flash as he smiled. 'I mean . . .' But her voice wobbled betrayingly.

He stopped walking and turned her to face him. 'If it's what I think it is, there's no hurry, you know. It's been a long exciting day. Anyway,' he smiled down at her again and touched her anxious face, 'it's still yesterday here, because we've crossed the International Date Line. Tomorrow's officially our wedding day in Western Samoa, date-wise.'

Clarissa's lips parted and she smiled uncertainly back at him. Then she sighed and rested her cheek on his shoulder for a moment. 'It's not that—I mean, I'm not really tired. And I won't have changed dramatically by tomorrow. The thing is, I'm really terribly inexperienced, although you might . . .'

'Oh, Clarry,' he interrupted softly, and took her into his arms, 'do you think I don't know that?'

'Well, I thought you might imagine I'd . . . well, experimented a little, but . . .'

'No. Nor is there anything terrible about it. In fact it appeals to me very much.'

'Does it?' she asked a little tremulously. 'I was worried I might make a fool of myself or . . . disappoint you. It's something I've never quite been able to think about,' she finished in a rush.

Rob was silent for a time, searching her face with a curious intensity. Then he said, 'I love you, Clarry. Just remember that.' And she thought there was an undercurrent of pain in his voice but couldn't imagine why, so she decided she'd imagined it.

She said herself, 'I love *you*, Rob,' and buried her face in his shoulder.

His lips moved on her hair. 'Then it will be all right, you'll see.'

All right? Clarissa thought, coming out of her memories briefly and staring at the flickering pattern of firelight on the wall opposite her bed. A tremor went through her body. How to describe being made love to by Rob? Or just being made love to for the first time, although she could never separate the event from the person in her mind. She hadn't cried because he hadn't hurt her, but she *had* been tense and just a little shocked—it was something she'd been unable to help. And she'd realised she'd been foolish not to make herself think more about the real intimacy between a man and a woman instead of allowing her thoughts to cut off at the proverbial bedroom door and imagine it would all take care of itself in a rose-coloured haze and with symphonic splendour. Because it was not as if she'd had an overly protected childhood in one sense—being brought up in the country, surrounded by animals, had seen to that. Nor was it that she didn't desperately want to respond to Rob's lovemaking—it was just, put simply, that being made love to, however gently, and suddenly realising what it meant to actually live with a man, had come as a shock.

And to her everlasting shame, she had burst into sudden tears *afterwards*, tears of confusion and despair because she was quite sure she *must* have disappointed him horribly, she was suddenly certain there was something wrong with her, and because, the strangest thing of all, she loved him ...

'Clarry, Clarry, don't,' Rob had murmured, rocking her in his arms. 'You should have told me I was hurting you.'

'You ... you weren't,' she wept. 'Not really. I just didn't know ... what to expect.'

'Then I must have let you down,' he said rather wryly.

'Oh no!' she'd gulped. 'It was the other way around.'

'What makes you say that?' he'd asked, holding her away from him.

'I just *know*.'

'Which only goes to show how little you do know, my darling Clarry. Can I tell you something? My first time was a real disappointment to me too.'

Clarissa had caught her breath and stared up at him with her eyes wide and her lips parted. 'Was it?' she whispered incredulously, then blushed hotly.

'Mmm. I won't bore you with the details,' he said very gravely but with his lips twitching. 'But I guess it's safe to say most people don't really know what to expect and a lot of first times are rather traumatic. Perhaps even more so when you've been brought up to be very modest, and anyway are that kind of person.'

'H-how did you know?' she had asked with a catch in her voice.

Rob had stared down into her confused eyes, then drawn her head into his shoulder, and she'd thought he'd said something like, 'The thing is, I should have known better.' But almost immediately, he had sat her up in his arms and said, 'Because I like to think I know you very well, my Clarry. The other thing is, it's almost always only a transitory state of affairs, especially if we can share it. And if only you'll give me a chance, I promise you matters will improve.'

'O-of course I will! I mean . . . I don't know what I mean, but I just felt . . . the thing is, will I improve?' Clarissa asked painfully.

'I can guarantee it. I have a reputation to maintain, you know,' Rob had said very seriously. 'How could I ever hold my head up again if my wife deserted me after our wedding night?'

'Oh, Rob,' she'd said, half-laughing, 'it wasn't you, it was me.'

'That's debatable,' he said enigmatically. Then he added abruptly, 'Clarry, if we still want to be with each other and if we take things slowly—I know I've said this before—it will be all right. Trust me. Do you?'

'More than anyone else in the world!'

'Then all *you* have to do is try to relax.'

She had tried, and to a great extent succeeded, so that that awful bout of shyness and nerves had almost become something to laugh about. And they had laughed a lot, although not about that, because somehow, Rob had managed to set their relationship on a dual footing so that the old and the new had begun to blend and so that they could enjoy lovely Western Samoa and also live together in harmony and in a growing, on Clarissa's part, sense of wonder.

She had come to enjoy coming back from a day of sailing and sightseing, dressed like a boy in shorts and a T-shirt and with her hair in a thick plait after having been as active as Rob, and then assuming a new role ... Dressing for dinner in something cool and pretty and discovering that for the first time in her life, her clothes, which she had in such abundance, thanks to her mother, had assumed a new meaning, just as her body had. Seeing a certain glint in his eye as they dined and coming to know with a not unpleasant little skip to her heartbeat what it meant ... That quite soon he intended to help her out of her pretty clothes and lay her on the bed and slide his hands over her body from head to toe in a way that left her feeling anything but boyish, that made her smooth, straight limbs feel incredibly soft and languorous, her golden skin tremble, and then part of her body that had never been revealed to anyone but Mrs Jacobs since puberty, her paler, pink-tipped breasts, her small, compact but rounded hips, the tops of her slender thighs, shiver in curious anticipation of the sensations Rob could arouse by touching her.

She had also become much bolder about touching him, and sometimes, when they were doing other things, she would catch her breath and experience an odd sensation at the pit of her stomach at the sight of his tall, lithe body, something not at all in keeping with their daytime relationship really. And that had been when it had begun to dawn on her that she was experimenting, or at least, slowly awakening to desire which she had just not understood the meaning of before, even in the days when she had wondered what it would be like to kiss Rob.

All this, but particularly his patience, the way he'd set out to show as much as anything else the lovely *fun* side of a relationship between two people who slept together, had doubled or trebled her regard for him, so that it had seemed like an unassailable force within her, her love for Robert Randall . . .

Yet it all came crashing down around me, Clarissa mused.

The firelight in her bedroom at Mirrabilla was less bright on the walls now, but the room was warm and serene.

If only I could *not* remember what came next, Clarissa thought, then with a restless movement of her head on the pillows, I might be able to *feel* warm and serene. But I should have known it was coming when Rob told me about buying my mother out on the plane trip home . . . I should have understood what it was all about, but I didn't. I had to be shown . . .

CHAPTER FOUR

'DON'T cry, Clarry,' said Rob gently.

'I'm not—I am. I'm just so sad to be leaving.'

'We could come back and have a second honeymoon. I take it you approved of your first?'

'Oh, Rob!'

'And you're not just crying because we're leaving?'

'No, I'm not. I'd love to have a second honeymoon with you, anywhere.'

He grinned and reached for her hand.

But some hours later, as their jet was banking for its final approach into Sydney, he said, 'Clarry, did your mother mention that she's sold her share of Mirrabilla to me? You and I are now joint shareholders.'

'No! Oh, Rob,' she turned to him anxiously, 'I feel . . . awkward about that. I . . .'

'There's no need to, Clarry,' he said soothingly. 'I think your mother would have sold anyway, and in the circumstances who better to than me?'

'Well,' she said slowly, 'I guess so. And she's never really *loved* Mirrabilla the way . . .' She stopped.

'The way you do? I know that. I thought we could live there. Would you like that? I'll probably have to be away from time to time, but then that would be the case wherever we lived. Perhaps I should have warned you before we married—about that.'

'Oh, I knew it would be like that! And if I've got Mirra . . .' Clarissa stopped again, self-consciously. Then she turned to him again urgently. 'Rob, I do still feel awkward about this. You didn't have to buy half

71

of Mirrabilla for me, because we got married . . . it . . .'

'Clarry,' he said steadily, 'for one thing, I love Mirrabilla too. Don't forget I grew up there as well. And for another, once it gets back on its feet, it will make a profit, so I'm only making a good investment—two good investments,' he added with a smile. 'In our future and in a place we both love, as well.'

'Rob, I do love you so,' she'd whispered. 'Thank you.'

Three months later, however, she was to remember those words, and her honeymoon, with a mixture of cynical irony and wretched despair. Who wouldn't, when you'd seen your mother and your husband in a passionate embrace and suddenly found a million little things whirling in your mind like a kaleidoscope to settle into a pattern going back for years . . . A pattern which only Clarissa Kingston had been too blind and too naïve to see or understand. And what she hadn't understood, had been explained in a conversation she'd overheard as she had stood rooted to the spot like a wraith in her long white nightgown just beyond the drawing-room doorway . . .

When she and Rob arrived back from Western Samoa, it was to discover that her mother had taken herself off on a round-the-world cruise. Clarissa was rather surprised but not unduly so. The excitement of going home, the heady prospect of having a real hand in helping to run Mirrabilla, the black and white pup Rob had presented her with to keep her company when he was away, which had somehow acquired the name of Mem—all this had kept her very busy and happy. Then another surprise had come along, and when she told Rob about it, he looked a shade rueful and remembered, 'Who said something about the best laid plans ganging agley? Do you mind?'

She considered gravely and discovered that she was a little apprehensive but mostly rather amazed and—well, proud. It seemed a very adult thing to be, to be pregnant. Besides, she got on well with young things. 'No. Do you?'

'Why should I mind?' he queried.

'I don't know. We'll be a real family now, won't we?'

'We certainly will.' He looked away over the verandah, his blue eyes distant.

'What is it, Rob?' Clarissa asked.

He looked back at her and smiled. 'I've never had a real family, just parts here and there. No, of course I don't mind, Clarry.'

'Oh, Rob!' she said a little tearfully, and went into his arms.

Then her mother arrived home, and she had only been at Mirrabilla one day, although she had proposed to spend a few days with them, when Clarissa had unwittingly witnessed that scene that was to stay in her memory for such a long time.

She had been pleased to see her mother, particularly looking so well. Narelle had been full of her cruise and especially talkative and vivacious—and quite stunningly attractive. Yet Clarissa hadn't quite got around to imparting her momentous news. Tomorow, I'll tell her tomorrow, she thought. Then Rob had come home and she'd wondered if he would mention it, but he hadn't.

It had been her momentous news that had sent her to bed rather early, however. Being pregnant had that effect on her, she had discovered, the effect of wanting to fall asleep at the end of the day like a child. But this day, she'd woken up before midnight, which was unusual because she normally slept like a child, right through, but she had woken up alone and decided to see what Rob was doing.

There was only one lamp on in the drawing-room, so she had stood at the drawing-room doorway in the shadows and her bare feet had made no sound. And as she'd watched, Rob had released her mother and pushed her away abruptly.

And her mother had staggered slightly, then dropped her head into her hands and started to speak in a low, choking voice but one that was perfectly audible to Clarissa.

'I *know* why you married her. It was for revenge, wasn't it? For the years ... oh God, what a mess!'

Rob's voice had been colder than Clarissa had ever heard it. 'Perhaps that too, Narelle. You did *toy* with me for years, didn't you? From the time I was about nineteen, to be precise, although even before that you ... looked. In fact you made my life hell. Even your own son began to wonder what was going on after that weekend he persuaded me to spend with him in Sydney for his birthday. But it was only a game to you, while I was a more or less penniless student and your part-time bloody butler, wasn't it? Then things changed ...'

'No! You don't understand—that had nothing to do with it! It was a sense of guilt, embarrassment ... despair that it could happen to me. A sense of disaster!'

'Narelle ...' Rob had made a curt gesture as if to cut her off, but she went on in a husky, tear-laden voice, 'Believe me, I didn't want it to happen and I knew you didn't either. You respected Bernard, you were so close to Ian, but all the same it did.'

'What's *happened*, Narelle, is that I've married Clarissa and this is all futile.'

'It wasn't futile a couple of minutes ago . . .'

'Yes, it was,' Rob had said grimly. 'Nor will it ever happen again. Even you surely couldn't want to cheat on your own daughter.'

'No,' Narelle had said hoarsely and agonisedly. 'I just want you to admit . . . the truth. Is that so much to ask? Just for my . . . own peace of mind, *please*!'

There had been a tense little silence. Then he'd said, 'I don't suppose you've stopped to consider that I might have married her to save her from being sold off to the highest bidder. That is what you had in mind, isn't it, Narelle?'

'No . . .'

'*Yes*,' he'd said through his teeth. 'Do you think I'm blind or stupid? You had her out on a platter tempting every eligible man in town, but with a price tag on her—*yes*, Narelle, don't you know it was the talk of the town? To marry Clarissa Kingston, first you had to get her mother's approval, and the one sure way to do that was to buy out her share of Mirrabilla, otherwise she'd influence her so beautiful daughter elsewhere.'

'Oh, Rob,' Narelle had said tormentedly, 'it wasn't like that. I wouldn't have forced her into anything! But she *might* have fallen in love with someone who . . . who could have. Don't you realise I was thinking of Clarissa all the time and desperately trying to save Mirrabilla for *her*? But I was running out of *time*. You know now that we were one step away from bankruptcy.'

'You could have come to me for help!'

Narelle had made a small dreary gesture. 'I happen to have some pride.'

Rob made a disgusted sound. 'Wouldn't it have been better to bury it than marry her off to God knows who, just to save face?'

'Rob,' Narelle had taken a deep, visible breath, 'I know Clarissa has always . . . meant something to you, but not in *this* way. She's only a *child* compared . . .'

'Well, at least she'll be safe with me!'

And that was when Clarissa had made a small sound and crumpled to the floor.

The curious thing, Clarissa later realised, was how she had handled things from then on. Because the moment her mother and Rob had revived her from the dead faint she'd fallen into, it was if she'd been wrapped in an insulating cocoon of some kind. She hadn't cried or felt particularly anguished. She had just stared at them both out of huge, darkened eyes, then turned away silently.

And it was quite a long time before she realised she'd lapsed into something like a state of shock, because it had stayed with her months and been a buffer that had prevented either of them from getting through to her. She had simply turned away from them. Not that her mother had stayed at Mirrabilla more than another day, but she had attempted to make an explanation—Clarissa hadn't heard a word of it. As for Rob, she had said to him the next morning '—don't please; I don't want to talk about it. I understand now, I really do. I'm only sorry I'm pregnant.'

Rob had studied her, his mouth set in a hard line, then he had closed his eyes briefly and said, 'I wish I could find the words to tell you that I'm not, Clarry.'

But she had turned away.

By the time she was about four months pregnant, Rob had told her that her mother would like to see her. And for the first time Clarissa had shown some emotion.

She'd started to shiver and gone white, and two days later she'd tried to run away.

But Rob had caught up with her only a few hours from Mirrabilla and brought her inexorably back. He had also been angrier than she'd ever seen him, and perhaps it was this that had finally elicited a spark of life from her.

'I didn't run away!' she cried at him. 'I can come and go as I please. I know you think I'm a child, but I'm *not*. And if I choose to support myself . . .'

'You're carrying on like a child, Clarry. You seem to forget you're *with* child yourself. And how the devil you expect to support both of you when you can't even look after yourself is a mystery to me. Just take a look at yourself! That alone should tell you how well you're supporting yourself and this baby. You're too thin, you've got great big shadows under your eyes . . . Whatever else has happened, Clarry, it's no fault of your baby, and no one should have to tell you that! Not if you're as grown up as you maintain.'

Clarissa stared at him.

'Oh, no, you don't,' Rob said grimly then, and taking her by the arm, he propelled her into the bedroom towards the mirror. 'It's time you stopped slipping away, Clarry, and faced some facts. *Look* at yourself!'

She did, properly, for the first time for ages, and turned away in despair. Then she put her hands on her stomach suddenly and frowned.

'What is it?' he asked urgently.

'I don't know,' she whispered, then felt it again, a small flutter. 'I think—I think it's moving.'

'Are you sure it's only that?'

'Yes. I . . . I've never really thought of it as a baby. Oh . . .' And suddenly the tears that had been held back for too long had started to flow.

Rob watched her silently, then took her hand. 'Promise me you won't do that again, Clarry.'

'No. I mean, no, I won't do it again, but it doesn't change ...'

'I know. But it's a start at least,' he said barely audibly.

He was right for the most part.

Clarissa started to take an interest in Mirrabilla again and the new manager, Cory Kessels, frequently came up to the homestead to discuss breeding stock and so on. She also started to take an interest in the running of the homestead, previously Mrs Jacobs' domain, but that good lady had been so thrilled to see Clarissa coming back to life, she wouldn't have minded if she'd turned all her routines upside down or imported a robot.

Mrs Jacobs had also been an ally of Rob's, despite having a pretty accurate idea of what had happened, and between them they had formed a watchful committee. 'A better day today, Mr Randall,' Mrs Jacobs would say, although she'd called him Rob for years. Or, 'A bit quiet today, Mr Randall, but it is very hot ...'

Two weeks before the baby was due, Rob and Clarissa moved to Canberra, and two days after the baby was due Clarissa went into labour. She wasn't sure whether she was glad or scared to death, but for the last month she'd felt slow and heavy, so she allowed a feeling of relief to gain the upper hand.

But as Rob was filling in forms at the hospital, a very efficient, starched-looking nurse beckoned her into the lift, and her heart started to beat heavily and she turned back and whispered in a frantic undertone,

'*Rob!*'

He was at her side immediately and waved away the nurse's protest with a curt, 'Check with Dr Forbes.'

'I was only going to say you can be with Mrs Randall as soon as we've ...'

'I'll wait outside the door until she's ready,' Rob said in a way which settled any further argument.

Dr Forbes was a large, friendly man, who, unbeknown to Clarissa, knew a great deal more about her than she had ever told him during the course of her pregnancy. Had she known, she might have understood the look that passed between Rob and the doctor when he arrived—one that suggested they knew each other rather well, which would also have surprised her.

It was a long, arduous labour, but Rob stayed by her side. And sometimes it seemed to her as if she was in her very early teens or younger as she gripped his hand and heard him say, 'Clarry?'

'Yes, Rob? How ... how am I doing?'

'Just great. I'm really proud of you.'

'Oh!' And she held his hand even tighter.

Until finally it was over and he was wiping the sweat and tears off her face.

'Is it ...?'

'It's a girl, Clarry. And you've been marvellous.'

'Only because of you ... Is she all right?'

'Perfect!' boomed Dr Forbes, and placed a tiny bundle in her arms.

Clarissa looked and believed him, and mopped her tears herself.

'What's this?' the doctor queried ruefully.

'Sometimes, Clarry cries when she's very happy,' Rob explained in an odd voice, and Clarissa turned to him to see that he looked inexpressibly weary.

She sniffed and smiled. 'I know what you're thinking of—Holly Kingston. But even she wasn't as beautiful.'

Rob closed his eyes as if relieved of a great weight. 'What will you call her?'

'I thought of Ian for a boy, but . . . does Sophie Randall sound all right?'

Three days later, however, Rob found Clarissa Randall weeping distractedly over Sophie Randall.

'What's wrong?' he asked.

'She . . . she's gone to sleep again!'

'Is that a disaster?' he asked warily.

'Yes! I've been trying to feed her for the last half hour and all she's done is sleep. Even when she's awake sometimes she—well, she doesn't seem to like me.' She looked at him tragically. 'I don't think I'm going to be a good mother at all!'

'Have you asked the Sister about it?'

Clarissa moved and winced. Her breasts were full and hard. 'I don't like to make a fuss, they've got a real rush on, and anyway, I *should* be able to manage!'

'Clarry,' he said in amused exasperation, but as the tears started to flow even more copiously, the amusement vanished and he said, 'Hang on, I'll be right back.'

He returned with no less a personage than the Matron, which caused Clarissa to flush in embarrassment and horror. 'I didn't—you shouldn't have—I'll get it right . . .'

'My dear Mrs Randall, I'm only sorry that this has happened, but unfortunately as sometimes *happens*, we've had a mixture of late and early births that's thrown our calculations temporarily askew. Babies do that, you know. Now what's this I hear about Sophie not liking you?'

'She doesn't—well, seem to suck very well. And she sleeps when she should be feeding and cries back in the nursery. I'm sure it's her!'

'Ah!' Matron said serenely. 'One of those, is she? I'll let you into a little secret, Mrs Randall—some babies just haven't read the rule books and four-hourly feeds mean nothing to them at all. So we'll put little Sophie on a demand system for the time being. As for the sucking—by the way, Mr Randall,' she turned to Rob, 'you can leave your wife to me now, she'll be quite fine, I promise you! Unless you'd like to sit in on a discussion about the techniques of breast feeding?'

'I think I might leave that up to you, Matron,' he said wryly.

After he'd gone, Clarissa tried to apologise for being such a nuisance, but the Matron waved her words away and said, 'I only wish I had more time to spend with mothers, especially young mothers, my dear. Now the first thing I'm going to preach to you is relaxation . . .'

Clarissa stayed in hospital for ten days, rather longer than normal, but Dr Forbes insisted on it and said he wished he could keep all his mums in for that long. In fact this was true, he did believe in a proper rest after a confinement, but it was more than that with Clarissa, although again she didn't know it.

But in those ten days, after that rather disastrous start, she came to know her baby and was finally able to go home feeling calm and confident.

Six weeks later, she said to Rob, 'I never thanked you for what you did for me when I was having Sophie.'

'You don't have to,' he shrugged.

'Yes. I don't think I would have got through it otherwise. Well, I suppose I would have, but it would have been much worse.'

'Clarry . . .' Something in his voice alerted her. He's going to suggest we—live together properly again, she thought. Could I? *How* could I . . .?

She jumped up, her mind flooded with images that made her heart pound and her mouth go dry. 'No . . .' she whispered and started to shake.

'Clarry!' He was beside her in one stride, holding her.

'No, Rob, I . . . I can't!'

'All right, you don't have to . . . Don't upset yourself.' And he held her gently until the shaking stopped.

'But what will we do?' she asked finally, helplessly.

'We don't have to do anything, Clarry. If you can be happy here with Sophie and the sheep, I'm sure that will be best for *her*.'

'Yes . . . yes. But what about you?'

'She might like to have her father around too!'

CHAPTER FIVE

Mrs Randall?'

Clarissa stirred and sat up sleepily. 'Oh, Mrs Jacobs,' she yawned, 'what's the time?'

'Ten o'clock.'

'What? Heavens above!' Clarissa exclaimed wryly.

'Are you feeling all right, Mrs Randall?' Mrs Jacobs asked anxiously. Clarissa had begged her to keep calling her Clarissa as she always had, but Mrs Jacobs had some very firmly rooted beliefs which included not using the familiarity of first names to employers however long you've known them. Which was a little odd, since she would have probably protected Clarissa's life at the expense of her own. But that was Mrs Jacobs, a lady of monumental loyalty and discretion. 'All that palava of the television show yesterday didn't upset you, did it?' she enquired.

'No! Oh ...' Clarissa blinked, recalling her disturbed night. 'Well, I did have some trouble getting to sleep. But then I must have passed out like a light, I guess.'

'Mr Randall said to leave you for a while. He had to go into Wollongong, but he'll be back tonight. Miss Patterson has gone back to Sydney. She said to thank you for your hospitality. Why don't you stay in bed if you're tired?'

'Because I'm not tired any more and I'm not sick,' Clarissa said firmly. 'Where's Sophie?'

'With Clover. I thought I'd check you out before I brought her in.'

Clarissa regarded Mrs Jacobs ruefully. 'Sometimes you treat me as if I'm no older than Sophie, Mrs Jacobs.'

'Well, I don't mean to, but . . .' Mrs Jacobs sighed.

'I know,' Clarissa said softly. 'There was a time when I . . . when it was probably appropriate. But it's not any more . . .' She stopped rather abruptly, remembering the tears she'd shed last night, the state she'd been in. Oh well, she told herself, flinching inwardly though, I'll just have to guard against those kind of lapses, won't I? Anyway, I haven't had one for ages.

After Mrs Jacobs had left her—to get dressed in peace, she said—Clarissa showered and donned a pair of jeans, low-heeled boots and a primrose-yellow jumper. She sat down at her dressing table and rather absently began to brush her hair. She noted the faint shadows beneath her eyes that hadn't been there yesterday, and wondered why it was that she felt quite calm this morning. Nothing had changed, nothing had gone away. She was still caught in a marriage that had turned into a nightmare . . .

'No, not that,' she said to her reflection. 'A trap for the unwary?' She shrugged. 'Perhaps. And it seems I have no option but to stay in it for the time being.'

Heavy footsteps sounded on the gravel outside her window, accompanied by Sophie's piping voice asking Clover why the birdies weren't singing.

Clarissa could imagine Clover taking his time about replying as the footsteps receded. He was an elderly man who had been Robert T. Randall's chauffeur for years. Now, at Mirrabilla, he performed a mixture of light duties, driving, some gardening and, in winter, tending the fireplaces in the homestead. And every time Clarissa asked him anxiously whether he wasn't doing too much, he replied that he was only happy to have something *to* do instead of being pensioned out to pasture like an old horse. He was also very much taken with Sophie and always answered her frequent questions at length and in detail.

Not that there was anybody at Mirrabilla who wasn't much taken with Sophie. As for Sophie herself, she loved Clover and Mrs Jacobs, adored her mother, but had one very important mission in life—to accord her tall father utter devotion. And this was something she took very seriously, even to the length of being able to recognise the sound of his car, so that every time the navy-blue Jaguar swept up the drive, Sophie would be the first out to greet him, dropping whatever was to hand and running as fast as her little legs would carry her.

In fact 'Daddy home' had become rather a catch-phrase in the household, used not only by Clarissa and Mrs Jacobs but even the daily help, whenever Sophie flashed by.

Clarissa put her brush down and got up to go over to the window where she watched Sophie and Clover disappear around the corner of the house, deep in discussion.

And she thought, what do I mean about having to stay in this marriage for the time being? Will there ever be a time when I can take Sophie away from Rob? For that matter, I haven't even thought about it for ages, until last night. I've even been ... happy. Happy to live side by side with him in a passionless but caring relationship—I could never accuse him of not being that. So what happened last night?

'Well, it did all come back,' she said aloud, and shivered suddenly. 'Perhaps because the night had grown cold ... Cold nights, lonely nights ... Was it that, more than talking about my mother and father? And Ian . . . No, not that. I could never feel that again, I think . . .'

But her gaze sharpened suddenly, and she realised that as she'd been talking to herself she'd been watching a figure stagger up the driveway—a figure growing more familiar with each painful step, a figure in a bright red suit but torn now and crumpled . . .

Clarissa turned with a gasp and ran out of her bedroom.

'Evonne!' she cried, coming out on the verandah. 'What's happened?'

Evonne Patterson lifted a face that was unusually pale even for her and slumped down on to the bottom step. 'I ran into a kangaroo, believe it or not,' she said breathlessly. 'It came right through the windscreen . . . Then I hit a tree. I waited, thinking someone would come along, but no one did, so I thought I'd better walk back . . .' She paused painfully, then lifted her skirt to show a nasty gash above one knee. 'I don't suppose I'd have bled to death, but all the same . . .'

'Oh, you poor thing!' Clarissa breathed. 'Hang on, I'll get help . . .'

'I'm sorry to be such a dreadful nuisance, 'Evonne said a little later when she was inside and being tended by Clarissa and Mrs Jacobs. 'I mean, having to get a doctor out . . .'

'He was holding a clinic in Holbrook anyway. And you're not being a nuisance!'

'In broad daylight, though, of all things . . . After spending the night here to avoid something like that!'

'Shh, Miss Patterson!' Mrs Jacobs admonished, 'don't fret about it.' She lifted her head. 'That could be Doctor now.'

'Now you'll stay with us, of course,' said Clarissa

after the doctor had stitched up Evonne's knee and pronounced her undamaged in any other way but had recommended that she take things quietly for the next few days.

'But . . .'

'Is there anyone in Sydney we should get in touch with?'

'No, but . . .'

'Then there's no one to take care of you, is there?' Clarissa said patiently.

'No. But I feel this is an awful imposition, though, Mrs Randall.' Evonne looked at her worriedly.

'No, it's not! In fact right now Mrs Jacobs and I will get you to bed, where you'll feel much more comfortable for the time being.'

'But I haven't got enough clothes or . . .'

'Oh, we'll find something. And Clover will organise something for your car. Now no more arguments, Miss Patterson!' Clarissa commanded with mock severity.

'I . . .' Evonne sighed, 'well, I do feel a bit groggy,' she confessed. 'Thank you very much, Mrs Randall.'

'I think I'd rather you called me Clarissa, Evonne.'

'She was incredibly lucky,' Clarissa said to Rob that night over dinner. 'The car's in an awful mess. Clover arranged for it to be towed into Holbrook for repairs.'

'How's she feeling now?'

'She's sleeping. She's slept for most of the day.' Clarissa reached for the apple sauce to put on her roast pork. 'She's very good at her job, isn't she, Rob?'

'Yes.'

'I was surprised to hear she didn't want to get in touch with anyone in Sydney. I thought she'd have a boy-friend at least. She's very attractive.'

They ate in silence for a while. The pork was delicious and the crackling crisped to perfection.

Then Rob said, 'Perhaps she's decided to be only a career woman. I got the feeling you didn't really like her, Clarry.'

Clarissa grimaced. 'It's not that, really. She makes me feel . . . I don't know, bumbling, by comparison. How did you guess, anyway?'

Rob looked up thoughtfully and twirled his crystal wine glass so that it sent out prisms of light across the polished surface of the table. 'I guess I should know you as well as anyone. For example, you're very talkative tonight.'

'Am I?' Clarissa looked fleetingly self-conscious.

'Yes. Not that I mind. I take it you've got over last night?'

'. . . Yes,' she said very quietly. 'Sorry about that.'

'It's not a question of being sorry.'

Clarissa moved restlessly and sipped her wine. 'I don't want to talk about it,' she said finally.

He shrugged, but those very blue eyes didn't leave her face.

'I . . .' Clarissa cast around in her mind a little desperately for something to say, and came up with something surprising but true. 'I think being able to dictate to Evonne today—sort of evened up the balance. I mean it demonstrated that there are some things *I'm* good at. I also felt . . . needed. How awful!' she finished with a comically rueful look.

He smiled slightly and remarked, 'Perhaps I ought to drive out and find a handy kangaroo to run into!'

Clarissa caught her breath and looked at him uncertainly—and was surprised to find the palms of her hands sweating.

'Don't worry, I'm not going to,' he said with a touch

of irony. 'But there are lots of things you're good at and areas where you're needed, Clarry. I don't quite understand why you should ... be rather euphoric about this. Oh, I do understand about people who give one an inferiority complex. I've met them too ... But you seem more alive than that would warrant, tonight.'

'I can't imagine you ever suffering from an inferiority complex,' she said a little drily, and then bit her lip, recalling her mother. Only I'm perfectly sure you got over that, Rob, she said to him mentally. She went on with an effort, 'And I'm only good at ... well, sheep and horses.'

'But you're very good at that, Clarry. Between you and Cory, Mirrabilla Stud is back where it once was again. You're also a good mother, despite your terrible doubts on that score once.' His lips twitched.

'Then again there are some things I'm very bad at,' she said abruptly, and flushed immediately; she couldn't imagine what had prompted her to say *that*.

He said, 'I can't think of one. Tell me about them?'

'I ... no, it doesn't matter.'

'Clarry.'

She pushed back her chair and stood up. 'No. Anyway, you know all about them.'

'All right, if it's going to upset you.'

'It's not!' she flashed at him. 'I'm ... sick and tired of being treated like an invalid!'

Rob lay back in his chair and simply watched her clutching the back of her chair, meditatively. And his silence was deafening—prove your point, in other words, Clarry ...

She sat down again and clenched her hands in her lap. 'I'm an awful wife, for one thing,' she said quietly.

'Perhaps I should be the judge of that.'

'I think,' she hesitated, 'you'd be the last person I'd consult.'

He raised his eyebrows. 'Oh?'

'Yes. You made it quite clear once that for you, I was more of a . . . a conservation project than anything else.'

'Clarry!' His voice was suddenly grim and he sat up.

But she said dispassionately, 'Oh, Rob, there are some things even I understand now. Our honeymoon, for example. It . . . I must have seemed terribly . . . tame to you.'

His eyes narrowed. 'Did I give you that impression at the time?'

'N-no.' Her voice faltered slightly. 'But at the time I didn't know any better,' she said.

'And now you do.' It was a flat statement, and the way he said it made her cheeks burn.

And a spark of anger lit her blue-grey eyes. 'I thought that was also made rather clear,' she said. 'I mean the difference between being . . . kind and gentle, and something that drives you, that . . . is occasionally impossible to resist, that has got into your blood . . .'

'I haven't laid eyes on your mother for over two years, Clarry. Do you mean that? I certainly resisted the urge to tear her out of the arms of her new husband, wouldn't you say? And incidentally, would you rather I hadn't been kind and gentle?'

'Yes—no . . . You *know* what I mean!' she said huskily. 'Even last night you said I was still a child then!'

'Actually, if you're talking about the way you slept with me, you did it as only you could have, with gallantry and style—since we're discussing these things academically, as I presume we are?'

She stared at him wordlessly.

'Didn't you enjoy your pork, Mrs Randall?' Mrs Jacobs enquired. Clarissa hadn't heard her come in and she coloured and said confusedly, 'Yes. Yes, I did, it was lovely. I just must not be very hungry. No, I'm feeling fine!' she added to Mrs Jacobs' anxious look, and jumped up again. 'I'll go and check on Evonne. Don't worry about dessert for me.'

Evonne was awake and had eaten a little.

'I'll be up and about tomorrow, I promise,' she said to Clarissa. 'I loathe being waited on, not to mention feeling bad about it from your point of view.'

Clarissa smiled. 'You're very independent, I think.'

Evonne stretched. 'I guess so. You—get that way when you've had to fend for yourself for most of your life.'

'Oh?'

'Well, my father deserted us. There were six of us and Mum found it very difficult to cope.'

'I'm not surprised,' Clarissa said frankly. 'So you . . .' She stopped.

'Mmm, I'm self-made. All the way from the back streets of Woolloomooloo.'

'I would never have . . .' Clarissa stopped again.

'Guessed it? I take that as a compliment, Mrs . . . Clarissa,' Evonne said quietly.

'I was afraid you'd think it was patronising.'

Evonne looked at her oddly, Clarissa thought. And then she said, 'Not coming from you. I think that's what's rather got to me about you.'

Clarissa looked startled.

Evonne grimaced. 'Must be the painkillers the doctor gave me,' she murmured, and turned her face away.

'I don't understand . . .'

Evonne sighed and turned back. 'In for a penny—— I think I've had a chip on my shoulder about you because you've had all the things I lacked. But not only that. You're so . . . it's hard to explain, but you're so above being patronising or snobbish. Too well bred, perhaps . . . and you don't make the terrible mistakes of taste I sometimes do, still. Like Sophie's dress.'

'Sophie's dress?' queried Clarissa.

'Yes. You know the one I wanted her to wear yesterday? The white frilly one with the blue sash? As soon as I saw her in her blue dungerees, I knew you were right. Only someone with awful pretensions and no taste would have dressed her up in that dress for a television show.'

Clarissa stared at her and then started to laugh softly. 'This is an amazing coincidence,' she said at last. 'Because I was just telling Rob that *you* gave *me* an inferiority complex because you were so efficient.'

That Evonne was jolted was obvious. She blinked and her mouth fell open. Then she started to laugh. 'My God,' she marvelled, 'that's crazy!'

'I think we're a crazy pair!' Clarissa agreed, then sobered. 'But I'm glad we've sorted it out. By the way, we found some clothes for you. They . . . belonged to my mother and they'll be a better fit than mine. She was about your height.'

'Your . . . mother's?'

'Yes. Oh, she never wore them. We found them still in their packages. She . . . er . . . had a thing about clothes. Now, would you like a nightcap? Or a book to read?'

'Amazingly, I think I'd like to go back to sleep!' said Evonne.

'Good,' said Clarissa. 'And Mrs Jacobs' room is just

two doors down if you need anything. Oh, incidentally,' she stopped at the doorway, 'I don't know about bad taste, but the real reason why I didn't want Sophie to wear that dress is because I have a thing about white dresses and blue sashes!'

Clarissa found Rob in her bedroom after she left Evonne.

'I just came to get an extra jumper,' she said. 'I thought of going for a walk.'

'Then I'll come too.'

Clarissa hesitated, but something about the set of his mouth stopped her from saying she'd rather go alone.

It was a clear, cold night, and they walked in silence for a while, Clarissa feeling nervous and ill at ease in case he wanted to continue their conversation from the dining table. She had regarded Mrs Jacobs' appearance as rather timely. Or perhaps it was just a cowardly way out, she mused, as she walked beside Rob in the moonlight.

'I've been thinking,' Rob said at last. 'Perhaps you're bored?'

Clarissa's lips parted. 'Bored?'

'Well, you haven't been off Mirrabilla for a long time, Clarry. Nor have you had any company, apart from us.'

'I don't mind that.'

'I know. But perhaps, for example, Evonne stimulates you. Had you thought of that?'

'You must be a mind-reader,' Clarissa said ruefully, and told him what Evonne had just told her. 'Isn't that odd—but perhaps you're right,' she said slowly.

'Then I think it's time you started to meet *more* people.'

Clarissa winced inwardly. Have I become a neurotic reluse? she wondered.

'How?' she asked.

'You could——' he paused, 'come to some of the social functions that I have to attend in Canberra and Sydney.'

'Oh, Rob, you know how I hate those things!'

'Clarry, I think there comes a time in your life when you have to regard socialising objectively. Doing it simply for the sake of doing it doesn't appeal to me either. But there are some times when you can't escape it—I can't, anyway—and if you can believe that there are in fact many, many interesting people out there, it helps. It's also true. And I'm certainly not asking you to indulge in a mindless round of social activity, but occasionally to accompany me when I think you might enjoy it.'

'Sophie . . .' Clarissa began, then stopped.

'Sophie is old enough now to cope with being left for the odd night or two. She has Mrs Jacobs, Clover and everyone else at Mirrabilla twisted round her little finger. Any more objections?'

Clarissa was silent. They'd stopped walking and were leaning on a fence. She pursed her lips and whistled, and presently hoofbeats sounded and a now matronly Holly Kingston with a gangly foal at her side cantered over a fold in the ground up to the fence to nuzzle Clarissa affectionately.

Clarissa stroked her nose, enquired after her baby and delved into her pocket for a carrot, but all the time she was thinking a little chaotically. What to say to this new development? The *last* thing she wanted to be doing—it was all very well to acknowledge that Evonne might have stimulated her ... Yet Rob sounded . . .? She cast an uncertain glance at him from beneath her lashes and thought he looked tall and forbidding and remote. She opened her mouth, then shut it again. What if she did do this, and did it well? Would she finally be able to persuade Rob that she was no longer a child?

'All right,' she said suddenly. 'Why not?'

Rob regarded her pensively in the moonlight, then he turned round and leant back against the fence rather wearily, with his arms folded.

'You work too hard, Rob,' Clarissa heard herself saying with a catch in her voice.

'So you told me last night.'

She said, 'Can't you try to break the habit?'

'It might just be the way I'm made.'

With a rather startling clarity, Clarissa found herself remembering a conversation she had had with Rob's father years ago, and she realised she had mistakenly assumed that inheriting his grandfather's empire would bring Rob the satisfaction he sought. Now, out of the blue, she asked herself suddenly what it really might have brought him. Power—yes, responsibility—definitely, masses of it, which he had not shirked as some might have said his father had. But what else? Well, very great wealth, obviously—but then she'd always had the feeling he would achieve sufficient wealth himself, but also the feeling that it wasn't terribly important to him . . .

And looking at his profile in the moonlight, she suddenly wondered if it hadn't brought him disillusionment too. If people fawned on him and disgusted him as her . . .

She caught her thoughts up apruptly, not ready to try and untangle what she thought of as the last mystery, subconsciously.

As for me . . . the thought tripped through her mind

and she was about to banish it as well, but something forced her to stop and examine it. For example, she'd been about as lukewarm as it was possible to be about this suggestion—have I got incredibly selfish? she marvelled. As well as reclusive, neurotic, recalcitrant . . . she shivered.

Rob straightened. 'Time to go in, I think.'

'I'm not too cold. I—actually it might be fun, Rob. I think I'll be looking forward to it.' Her voice trembled slightly, but she was smiling.

He searched her face intently for a moment. Then he put a casual arm about her shoulders, but all he said was, 'I'm glad.'

In bed that night, Clarissa discovered her thoughts taking another turn.

Or rather, following on her earlier train but with a sudden leap forward that made her wince and bite her lip. Because she'd never before really stopped to wonder how much this marriage was costing Rob in a physical sense. Had all the care and attention he'd surrounded her with, for example, included his staying faithful to her?

'For over two *years*?' she whispered.

She sat up, then lay back agitatedly. In fact she had wondered about this before, but not from Rob's point of view. She occasionally and cynically assumed it probably would have happened anyway, and deliberately cut her thoughts off at that point.

Now she found herself wondering all sorts of things. Who? Or was it a succession of women? Or . . . no, she didn't believe that any more, but really, who could blame him if he had . . . strayed, for want of a better word?

She sat up again and thought with a peculiarly

haunting chill—could one blame *me*? Surely not! After all, I was the ... what was I? The innocent party?

But as that familiar feeling of tension began to mount within, she deliberately took hold. I just can't let this keep happening to me, she told herself. I just can't.

And perhaps the rigours of two rather different days helped, because she lay back with an exhausted sigh, and presently fell asleep.

Rob had another surprise for her over breakfast. He said idly, 'I've been thinking. Now that you and Evonne have come to like and understand each other ...' He stopped and waited as if for Clarissa to contradict him.

She thought for a moment, then said, 'Well—yes?'

'Then she might be some help to you as *your* secretary,' he shrugged, 'companion for a time.'

Clarissa's mouth dropped open. 'What do you mean?' she asked.

'Wouldn't it,' he said as if choosing his words with care, 'be a help to have another woman to ... discuss clothes with, parties, events, the people you might meet and their backgrounds—to be able to not only talk about it but accompany you on any shopping trips etc., and also someone who is conversant with the business world, as Evonne undoubtedly is, but not only mine—the world of big business, you might say?'

Clarissa blinked several times. 'I ... I suppose so,' she said at last. 'But she's your press secretary, for one thing. For another, she might ... well, object to being sort of seconded to me. And she might find the whole idea insanely boring.'

'I'm sure I could replace her temporarily,' he

assured her. 'She also has a rather bright future with us which I don't suppose she's unaware of.'

'If you think I'd enjoy having her ... company, because she's afraid to say no on account of jepoardising her bright future with you, I wouldn't!' Clarissa told him indignantly.

Rob lay back in his chair and regarded her amusedly. 'I wasn't trying to say that. I meant she would probably quite sensibly regard it as another facet of her job—even a perk.

Clarissa stared at him nonplussed.

'I also happen to know,' he added, sitting up, 'that there are some things about Mirrabilla that fascinate her.'

'What things?'

'Everything that the family have for years regarded as memorabilia,' he said with a grin. 'Like your great-great-grandfather's diary.'

'How do you know this?'

'The night before last, after the television crew had left and you'd gone to tuck Sophie in, she mentioned to me that the place was packed with history, most of it just lying about, which she thought was a crying shame, and that it should at least be catalogued and better preserved.'

Several succeeding expressions chased across Clarissa's face, but finally she laughed. 'That sounds like Evonne,' she said wryly. 'Do you—do you think she'd be interested in doing that?'

'She wouldn't have mentioned it if she didn't have an interest in that kind of thing.'

'You're right, I guess,' Clarissa said slowly.

'And,' Rob pointed out, 'as we have established, she has no ties in Sydney.'

'I ...' She bit her lip and looked confused.

'But you don't have to make a decision right away,' Rob said mildly. 'You're going to have her company for a few days by the look of things, so why don't you just . . . bear it in mind? I'll be in Canberra for the next few days, by the way.'

'Oh. Well, all right, I might just do that,' Clarissa said lamely, and with the feeling that her life had suddenly and inexplicably started to speed up like a film on a runaway movie projector.

'Don't look so worried,' Rob said quietly. 'Whatever else has happened, do you really think I don't have your best interests at heart, Clarry?'

'I . . . no,' she said huskily.

But she thought later, after he had left, that although his suggestions had been made so—almost casually, she sensed a purpose within him that could not be denied any more. The iron fist in the velvet glove? she mused, then found herself wondering what more he would expect of her now that he was . . . sort of setting her back on the road again. Is that the right way to describe it? she asked herself. Or is he saying to me, if you're so sure you can stand on your on two feet now, prove it?

Perhaps I do need to pove it, if not to him, to myself?

Two days later, Clarissa said to Evonne, 'I've had this thought.'

They were sitting on the verandah having afternoon tea. Mem lay at Clarissa's feet and Sophie was playing happily with her building blocks. It was a cold but bright afternoon and they were protected by the house from the wind that struck through one as if it was blowing straight off Mount Kosciusko to the southeast. Clarissa had spent most of the morning on horseback as she and Cory and Mem had helped move sheep to new paddocks with winter feed, and she was liberally anointed with lanolin, especially on her cheeks, lips and hands to ward off the chapping effect of the wind. Which made her tea taste odd.

But she had used the morning spent beneath a vast, clear blue sky to do other than herd sheep, which she could do in her sleep anyway. She had found herself thinking clearly and objectively as her saddle had creaked and the dust had boiled. And Mem had barked and cajoled and heckled and leapt lightly across those woolly backs—Mem was going to be a champion sheepdog.

'You had this thought?'

'Yes. Evonne . . .' Clarissa paused and glanced at Evonne. She was smartly but casually dressed in a pair of tweed pants and thick cyclamen-pink sweater that suited her complexion. Yesterday, Clarissa had told Evonne she would like her to have her mother's clothes which suited and fitted her so well. Evonne had begun to protest rather stiffly, but she had told her her mother had no use for them now and anyway never wore clothes more than two seasons old. Then she'd been struck by a thought and laughingly asked Evonne if she was being patronising instead of just practical as she'd thought. Evonne had hesitated and then had said, wryly, 'Practical—that was just my chip showing.' 'Evonne, would you care to be my secretary-stroke-companion for a little while?'

Evonne's dark eyes widened and she spluttered on a mouthful of tea. 'Say that again?'

Clarissa did, and went on to explain. She finished by saying, 'I've been out of things since before Sophie was born, you see. And even so, I never knew much about the Randall empire. And I think Rob would like me to help out on the social side now that Sophie is no longer a baby really. I'm not a natural socialiser, though, firstly, and secondly I suspect I've become rather rusticated. Is there such a word?'

'I don't know.' Evonne smiled, then sobered. 'You were perfect for Moira Stapleton.'

'But I was very much on my home ground.'

'Have you discussed this with Mr Randall? Naturally I couldn't . . .

'It was his idea,' Clarissa told her.

'Oh.'

Clarissa bit her lip and wondered if she shouldn't have let Rob speak to Evonne first. 'Evonne, he also said you had a very bright future with him, and that this would only be temporary. I know he meant it, but I suppose it sounds a little strange to you. I can guarantee that there would be no . . . no . . . I mean, if you decided not to, if it didn't appeal to you, I know Rob wouldn't hold it against you. Neither would I. So . . . what do you think?'

Evonne stared past her with narrowed eyes and Clarissa wondered what she was thinking. Was it naïve to put an employee of Rob's in this position?

She thought Evonne sighed then, but as those dark eyes focused on her, the other girl said with a faint smile quirking her lips, 'If you had any idea how I've longed to take a short sabbatical—a contradiction in terms, probably, but if you know what I mean—and spend it doing something like this. I'm addicted to Australiana, I must warn you!'

'So Rob thought,' Clarissa said with a grin. 'And you know, apart from Mirrabilla, this is a marvellous area for it. We had our own bushrangers—not as famous as Ned Kelly, but Mad Dan Morgan used to haunt this area—Holbrook, Henty and Culcairn. And there's the Woolpack Inn Museum in Holbrook. It was originally a pub that opened in eighteen-thirty something, but now it houses a terrific collection of antiques. Did you know Holbrook was originally called Germantown? Well, it was until the First World War, then it was renamed after Commander Norman Holbrook who won a V.C. in the Dardanelles, I think. That's a replica of his submarine in the main street.'

'My dear Clarissa, you're a mine of information, and you might never get rid of me! As to the other side of it, perhaps I *could* be of some assistance. I . . . occasionally I've . . . well, not deputised for you exactly, but I have found myself at a few functions . . . er . . . dealing with the wives.'

It was Clarissa's turn to say, 'Oh?'

'Do you mind?' asked Evonne with her usual directness.

Do I? How could I? 'No! Clothes,' Clarissa said succinctly. 'Not that I'm like my mother, but I haven't had any new, fashionable ones since I was a teenager. Just in case I haven't outgrown that image, it might be wise to get some new ones. Will you come to Sydney with me and help me to consolidate the image of a woman of the world, not to mention a matron nowadays?' She glanced at Sophie whimsically.

Evonne laughed. 'You must be the least matronly matron I've ever laid eyes upon! Yes, I'll come.'

Sophie pricked up her ears then, and at the sound of a car, she was off, scattering blocks.

Clarissa and Evonne followed with Evonne saying, 'Daddy come, by the sound of it!'

Rob got out of the Jaguar, stretched and said, 'Well, ladies, what have we here? A reception committee?'

He swung a delighted Sophie up into his arms and Clarissa tilted her face for his customary kiss.

'We've got something to tell you!' she said almost immediately, and triumphantly.

He blinked and Evonne laughed. 'Perhaps we ought to give Mr Randall time to unwind first,' Evonne suggested.

'Daddy home!' Sophie said proudly and tenderly. 'Daddy tired?' she asked, her blue eyes round with concern.

'Not too tired for you, baby,' her father smiled, and Clarissa thought with a sudden pang that Sophie was more considerate of him than she was. And Evonne . . . I wonder how she would welcome a man home, *her* man.

'Actually I couldn't stand the suspense,' said Rob.

'Well, Evonne has agreed to what . . . to what you suggested, Rob,' Clarissa told him.

Rob looked at her first, with his eyebrows raised, and then at Evonne, who returned his look soberly and very directly, which made Clarissa suddenly wonder if Evonne *knew* more about her than she'd ever told her.

But Rob said then, 'That's excellent. Particularly as the seventy-fifth birthday of Randall's is coming up shortly. Well, ladies, I think we should go inside and toast this—alliance. what do you reckon, Sophie Randall!'

CHAPTER SIX

'WHAT do you think?'

'Mmm . . . not quite you. Too old.'

'I don't want to look too young, Evonne!'

'Clarissa, someone will remind you of those words one day! Take care what you say. You know what it is about this outfit, it's the colour. Pastels suit you better.'

'I agree with you, Miss Patterson,' the vendeuse put in. Clarissa could think of no other way to describe her, because she looked as if she'd stepped straight out of the pages of *Vogue* if not the portals of Christian Dior, Paris, although they were in Double Bay, Sydney. 'Cornflower-blue, maize, pale greys, hyacinth-pink, peppermint-greens—possibly black,' she added. 'But bright red, no. That's your colour, Miss Patterson.'

'Oh well,' Clarissa said philosophically, stepping out of a red dress with matching jacket, 'I'll be guided by you two. The thing is I'd like just one more outfit. Then I'll go home happy!'

'Let me show you this little number, Mrs Randall . . .'

Home in this instance was the Regent Hotel in George Street. And Clarissa flopped exhaustedly into a chair and kicked her shoes off, surrounded by a sea of packages. 'Tea,' she said laughingly. 'That's what I need, a cup of tea!'

'Personally, I need a strong drink,' decided Evonne.

'Oh, Evonne, you've been super today! Let's have one, then!'

'I've really done nothing, but how about a glass of white wine?'

'Lovely. Yes, you have. You've taken me to the most divine shops and helped me spend a small fortune of Rob's money, which I don't regret in the slightest. And they all seemed to know you!'

Evonne grinned and handed her a glass. 'Now that I can afford to, I shop for quality, but in reality very frugally. I mean, one good outfit from those kind of boutiques lasts me for a good long time. But I must tell you, Clarissa, you have been a real feather in my cap and will probably save me some money in the future.'

'What do you mean?'

Evonne shrugged and sipped her wine. 'Having brought Mrs Robert Randall into their orbit.'

'I . . . oh! Will you get a commission?'

'Not exactly. But some rather discreet reductions, perhaps, from some of them. So you see there's no need to thank me.'

Clarissa had to laugh. 'You're very honest, Evonne.'

'Too honest?' Evonne queried.

'No! For heaven's sake, don't change! I wonder if Rob will be home tonight?'

'Er . . . no, there was a message at Reception when I collected the key. He's tied up in Broken Hill.'

'Never mind,' Clarissa said cheerfully. 'I'll shout you dinner. What about tomorrow? What have we planned?'

'A visit to the beauty parlour so that we both look our very best for your first social engagement tomorrow night, Mrs Randall! Other than that, we could relax. Shall we go through the triumphs of today?'

'Yes, let's!'

And soon the lounge of the suite was strewn with clothes, lingerie, shoes, belts, purses, scarves, sweaters . . .

'Clarissa? Are you all right?'

Clarissa turned from the window. It was the following evening and she was dressed and ready for her first social function, as Evonne had put it.

She wore a long, clinging gown of shimmering silver and white with a matching collarless jacket, high silver shoes, and was clutching a silver mesh evening purse. The beauty parlour had wrought a minor miracle of grooming, she thought, and had experimented with several discreet make-ups before hitting on one that was a miracle of understatement yet highlighted her best features like her eyes, and they had carefully instructed her how to do it herself. Her hair had been trimmed but still came to below her shoulders, yet it had an added fullness and body thanks to the blow-dry they'd given it.

So that she looked young and fresh but elegant and perfectly finished. Exactly as she'd hoped to look.

It was not a big affair they were attending—so Evonne had briefed her. A dinner-dance, in fact, at another premier hotel, but there were likely to be some captains of industry and commerce present and their ladies. It was a pre-dinner, apparently, for the three-quarter centenary of Robert T. Randall's empire. Evonne was attending it too, and looked unusually demure in dull yellow taffeta.

'Yes, I'm fine. You shouldn't have to spend frugally, Evonne. Doesn't Rob give you a dress allowance?' Clarissa asked jerkily. 'Where *is* he, I wonder? Aren't we due to leave in about twenty minutes?'

'He'll be here soon,' Evonne said soothingly. 'Probably just caught up in traffic. Would you . . . like a drink?'

'No.'

'Clarissa . . .'

'Evonne, I can't go through with this,' Clarissa said agitatedly. 'I should never have come to Sydney. I was quite happy back at Mirrabilla. I think . . . I think you'll have to deputise for me again . . .' She swallowed rapidly and to her horror, felt tears starting in her eyes.

'Clarissa!' Evonne said urgently, then put her hands together as she changed tack deliberately. 'Clarissa— rather, may I call you Clarry? I feel as if I know you well enough to, not to mention admiring you and being quite *certain* you can handle this . . .'

'You don't know me at all, Evonne. How could you when I don't even know myself very well? But I do know I was a fool to think . . . to,' Clarissa swallowed again and found her heart pounding, 'to . . . I don't know any of them. And I haven't seen Rob for days! How can he expect . . .' She stopped abruptly with tears now streaming down her face as the outer door to the suite opened and closed and Rob walked into the lounge.

'Why, Clarry,' he said as he pulled off his tie, 'you look sens . . . What's the matter?' he asked sharply then, and glanced at Evonne.

She made the tiniest motion of helplessness and then, perhaps at some unspoken interchange between her and Rob, walked through into the second bedroom and closed the door.

'I can't . . . I just can't come tonight, Rob,' Clarissa told him, and there was pure panic in her voice and eyes. 'Oh, Rob, you were right about me all along!'

'Clarry, no,' he said, and walked over to her to take her into his arms.

'Yes!' she wept into his shoulder.

'No—listen to me.' He picked her up and sat down on the couch with her. 'This is my fault. I meant to be back much earlier, but something's come up that's very serious. In fact it was the only thing I would put in front of being with you today. Clarry?'

'It doesn't matter, it doesn't . . .'

'Don't you even want to hear about it?'

'I . . .' She gripped his sleeve tightly, then forced herself to take a steadying breath. 'Yes, if you want to tell me, but it's not that . . .'

'I think it is, but why don't you judge for yourself? All our mining operations are threatened with a strike.'

Her lips parted. 'All?'

'Yes.'

'You mean a general miners' strike?'

'No. Only Randall's,' he said a shade ironically.

'Rob! That sounds awful!'

'It's not pleasant, not for anyone. It's also rather difficult to be in my position. I now part-own some of the mines I once worked in, I know many of the workers, I've worked alongside them, I know their families. But I'm on the other side of the fence now. The other thing is, my grandfather was always very proud of his record in labour relations. So, and especially in this seventy-fifth year, it would be unfortunate if *I* blew that record. And I expect all sides are watching with great interest to see how I handle this trouble, but not only that, there are some who wouldn't mind if I fell flat on my face. Even within Randall's, a few people still regard me as the boy from the bush or think I was too young to take over right from the top.'

Clarissa stared into his blue eyes with more intensity than she had for years, and felt a dull little ache within that she should have been so blind and oblivious. Things hadn't been easy for Rob either, but she'd been too caught up with herself to even bother.

She rubbed her face, then looked at her fingers and grimaced. 'I might have to start again,' she said in a gruff little voice. 'But then you've still got to get changed. Would you like a drink first? I'll ask Evonne to ring ahead and explain that we'll be late.'

Rob seemed about to say something, but in the end he just kissed her lips lightly, and she rested against him briefly, feeling an uprush of unusual warmth and tenderness.

'. . . How do you do? I'm so sorry we're late . . .'

'. . . How do you do? Yes. I'm Rob's wife. Well . . . um . . . it's not that he's been hiding me, but we do have a little girl and . . . oh yes, I think it is important to be with your children as much as you can. How do you do . . .'

The gathering was about sixty strong and the elegant room hummed with conversation and something more, an almost tangible aura of power. Even Clarissa, who had seen many a famous face pass through Mirrabilla during her mother's reign, was surprised at how many there were on this one occasion.

But some of the faces were familiar for other reasons, such as Bill Prentice, a long-time friend of her father. And he pounced on her delightedly and told her she was growing up to be a 'right chip off the old block'. A self-made man and proud of it, Bill Prentice had never tried to hide his humble origins, rather to the chagrin of his wife.

Clarissa found herself seated next but one to Mrs
Prentice with a thin, stern-looking man between them
and a pixieish-looking man on her other side. Rob was
some way down the table with one of the most
beautiful women Clarissa had ever seen next to him.
Evonne was diagonally opposite her.

'How is your dear, dear mother, Clarissa?' Mrs
Prentice boomed, cutting out the man between them
as if he didn't exist. Everything about Mrs Prentice
was on a grand scale and it was no surprise that this
large deep voice should emerge from a visibly
restrained chest of massive proportions clothed in
mustard embroidered crêpe.

'How now, brown cow,' the pixieish gentleman on
Clarissa's other side murmured.

'I beg your pardon?'

'She should have been an opera singer. Would have
made a magnificent Brunnhilde—she's waiting for an
answer.'

'Oh . . . very well, thank you, Mrs Prentice. She's
. . . er . . .'

But fortunately Mrs Prentice decided to regale
Clarissa with some of the cherished memories she had
of her dear, dear mother—Clarissa's not her own—
and for the next five minutes it was impossible but also
unnecessary to get a word in edgeways. Then she
smiled graciously at Clarissa, backed a notch and gave
her full attention to the gentleman between them, who
suddenly looked not stern but nervous.

'Tell me about sheep, Mrs Randall,' the little man
on her right said into the vacuum.

'Sheep, sheep——' Clarissa repeated rapidly,
wrenching her mind from her mother and the insane
thought that all Mrs Prentice lacked was a helmet with

little horns. Then she became aware that her companion, whose name now escaped her and anyway hadn't meant much to her, was regarding her with a benevolent but slightly patronising twinkle in his eye which she didn't understand but which put her on her mettle.

'Sheep fall into two basic categories,' she said casually. 'Those that you eat and those that you wear. Those that you eat are the larger-bodied sheep— Leicester's Lincoln, Romney Marsh, Shropshires and Southdowns—and their wool is coarse. Whereas Merinos have very fine wool, very little meat by comparison and, above all else, the ability to survive virtually in the desert. Cross-breeding has occurred, naturally, mainly in the attempt to refine the coarser wool, but since the advent of freezing and exporting meat they've come into their own right, the coarse wool breeds. Other than that,' she cast the little man a laughing look, 'most people will tell you that sheep just have no character! You get dogs and cats and horses and even bullocks and pigs you can tell fine stories about, but sheep stories are about as the thick on the ground as gold nuggets in Pit Street!'

The little man laughed with genuine amusement and something like admiration, and they then had a lively discussion about the general state of the wool industry, including some of its problems such as the wide comb issue.

Until Clarissa said, 'By the way, I'm sorry, but I missed your name.'

'Roger Cartwright, Mrs Randall. How do you do? I must say I'm pleased to meet you—you've come as a bit of a surprise. Er . . . Brunnhilde is about to claim your attention again.'

'How am I doing?' Clarissa asked Evonne in the powder-room after dinner.

'I would say fantastic.'

Clarissa grinned. 'You don't have to say that.'

'But you're enjoying yourself?'

'Well, I've had a few strange encounters, but yes, I am. Did you know about this miners' strike, Evonne?'

Their gazes caught and held in the mirror. Evonne put her lipstick away and touched her hair. 'Yes.'

'Why didn't you tell me?'

'I wasn't sure Mr Randall wanted you to know,' said Evonne snapping her purse closed and looking back directly at Clarissa.

'Oh,' Clarissa said thoughtfully.

'Was I wrong?' Evonne enquired.

'No—well, no. You probably summed up the situation perfectly from my point of view. But I think it's time I did know more of what's going on, and not only the social facts but the hard facts.'

Evonne was silent for a moment. Then she said with a slight smile, 'Very well, Clarissa.'

'Oh, I didn't mean to sound pompous!' Clarissa said ruefully. 'And anyway, I'm sure you must think I'm an odd wife, but,' she shrugged, 'I mean to be a better one now.' In one sense, she thought with a sudden pang.

As they were leaving the powder-room the tall, striking woman who had been beside Rob went in, and Clarissa glanced at her and frowned.

'Who is that?' she whispered to Evonne as the door closed. 'I'm sure I know her face. Isn't she gorgeous?'

'That's Lineesa Marchmont—David Marchmont's wife,' Evonne told her. 'She used to be a top model— Lineesa Creighton.'

'Oh, of course! And I've heard of the Marchmonts, who hasn't! Are they ... very social?'

'Not really. I believe Lineesa has two children now and she's mostly content to live at their place on the Hawkesbury near Wiseman's Ferry. Although I believe she writes poetry and short stories.'

'Do point him out to me—David Marchmont.'

'As a matter of fact he's the tall fair man talking to your husband right now. Two exceptional examples of the male animal, wouldn't you say?'

Clarissa blinked. 'I would say—yes,' she conceded, and looked quizzically at Evonne. 'Are you trying to tell me something?'

'Only that you're very lucky! Do you ever spare a thought for all us countless spinsters eating our hearts out for the likes of Robert Randall and David Marchmont?' Evonne adopted a look of such mournfulness, Clarissa had to smile.

'I couldn't even begin to imagine you as a poor spinster, Evonne,' she said. 'And talking of male animals, I happened to notice that the one sitting next to you at dinner wasn't a bad example either, and what's more, to put it simply, couldn't take his eyes off you. Whereas I,' she went on, 'had Brunnhilde next but one to me and a strange little man on the other side who gave me the third degree about wide shearing combs! Who is he, by the way? He said his name was Roger something . . .'

'Oh God, did he?' Evonne stopped and looked at Clarissa urgently. 'You mean he really . . .'

'He really did. Why? What's wrong?'

'He's the special correspondent of the *Canberra Times*! You could end up in print tomorrow, Clarry!'

'But that's not fair! I had no idea who he was!'

'What did you say?' asked Evonne.

'Exactly what I thought . . .'

'Clarry? Evonne?' Rob had strolled up to them and

was standing looking down at them with a curious smile. 'You look like two naughty little girls caught robbing the sweet shop! What is it?'

Evonne told him. 'Relax, girls,' he said with a broadening smile. 'He's spoken to me and asked my permission to mention in his column that Bernard Kingston's daughter is not only beautiful but intelligent and amusing.'

'Well,' laughed Evonne, 'I think this calls for a celebration—a drink, in other words! Because you're made now, Clarry, I would say. Wouldn't you?' she appealed to Rob.

But Rob only raised his eyebrows quizzically.

The rest of the evening passed amazingly quickly and with no more alarms or serious nerves for Clarissa. She danced with a variety of people and got to meet David and Lineesa Marchmont. In fact they were to form one of her most lasting impressions of the party. She was introduced to them separately and liked them both, but it was what she saw later in the evening that made such an impact on her, although she didn't realise it at the time.

They had been apart for some time, the Marchmonts, talking to different people, with different groups, dancing with others. Then Lineesa came back to David's side and although he was deep in conversation, Clarissa, who was standing nearby, got he strongest impression that he knew his wife was there before she said anything, and before he'd seen her. Because he moved his hand and she slid hers into it, and only then did he turn. They looked into each other's eyes for a few moments, so deeply that Clarissa suddenly found herself covered in gooseflesh.

Then David Marchmont excused himself quietly

and led his wife on to the dance floor and took her into his arms, and it was the most intensely private coming together of two people in the middle of a crowd Clarissa had ever witnessed, in the sense that, for them, it seemed as if there was no crowd, just the two of them . . .

She turned away abruptly, wondering that she should be feeling a little odd, as if she was trying to understand some hidden truth or meaning or answer a question she hadn't heard asked.

She wasn't allowed to dwell on it for long yet, but at the end of the night when she and Rob and Evonne were back at the hotel, instead of being high on a triumphant evening, she found herself suddenly feeling exhausted and deflated.

'I think . . . I think I'll go to bed,' she said as Evonne was making coffee for them. 'I don't think I'll bother with coffee, thank you. I . . .' She stopped and bit her lip as something else hit her. The suite had two bedrooms, one of which Evonne was occupying. The other did have twin beds, but it was years since she and Rob had shared a bedroom. Tonight there was no alternative, obviously, but the thought of it was suddenly monumental.

Did Rob guess what she was thinking? she wondered later. Because he had come across the lounge to her then and put his hands on her shoulders, and kissed her lightly on the forehead. And said, 'You were terrific Clarry. Thank you.'

'I didn't do much,' she had whispered.

'Yes, you did. Look, why don't you get ready for bed? I'll look in in a while. Would you mind very much if I commandeered Evonne for a short time now? I've got a briefcase full of notes she might be able to help me put into some sort of useful order.'

'No! I mean no, I don't mind, but aren't you both tired too?'

'I might sleep easier if I know it's done. Evonne?' He turned to her.

'I don't mind,' said Evonne. 'I usually need to unwind before I can go to bed anyway. And if it's ammunition you have in your briefcase, to help avert this strike, I'd like to.'

'All right,' Clarissa said slowly. 'Goodnight, Evonne. Thank you—for everything,' she added huskily but warmly.

And Evonne had done something quite uncharacteristic. She had come across the room and hugged Clarissa. 'It was a pleasure.'

When Rob looked in, Clarissa pretended she was asleep. In fact she wasn't far off it, so the pretence wasn't difficult. Why she should have pretended was not quite clear to her drowsy mind, but when she heard Rob walk quietly out of the room, she also heard Evonne ask, 'All right?' and his reply, 'Yes. Asleep.' Then the door closed and she heard no more. But on top of a brilliant but bewildering day came the painful thought that they might have been talking about a child suffering from overtiredness and reaction. She thought dimly that that was why she was pretending to be asleep—they were at least partly right. She could think no more, she was too confused, too tired, too . . .

She fell asleep.

She woke just before dawn and lay for a while watching the outlines in the room beginning to define. The curtains on one window weren't quite closed, and anyway, her eyes were adjusting to the darkness. She could make out, gradually, Rob's outline on the other bed. He was lying on his side, facing away from her, breathing deeply and evenly, with one arm under the pillow, by the look of it.

And as the wintry dawn light seeped in, Clarissa shivered. Not because she was cold but because she felt intensely lonely all of a sudden as she remembered that Rob mostly slept on his side.

And she lay there thinking about it and trying not to but finding her thoughts, her imagination, too powerful to resist . . .

She remembered how she had often slept curled up beside him, curved into his body, protected by his shoulder looming over her, his hand—the one not under the pillow—resting on her hip or that arm slid beneath her breasts. It had been what she'd liked best, she thought with a piercing sense of clarity. To be held loosely like that in peace and serenity. To be freed of the weighty obligations of sex which she hadn't thought she was much good at, but to be gathered and held in affection and warmth had moved her and succoured her. To wake up and to feel his warm skin against hers and the width of his shoulders behind her narrow ones, the longer length of his legs, to plait her fingers through his—she'd loved that.

Then the thought crossed her mind that she could get up and slip into his bed, and she trembled and felt her cheeks grow warm and her heart start to beat faster, so fast the she felt as if she was suffocating and as if that awfully familiar sense of confusion and fear was claiming her.

She did get up, very quietly, but slipped into the bathroom to have a shower.

Rob hadn't moved when she came out, and on an impulse she slid on a pair of jeans and a thick sweater, then left the suite as silently as a wraith. Evonne's bedroom door was closed and there was no sound from within.

She came out into George Street and started to walk aimlessly. There was very little traffic but quite a few pedestrians in the dark city canyons, and as she approached Circular Quay, she encountered more and more and realised they were early workers coming up from the underground stations and off the ferries that crisscrossed Sydney Harbour. They were mostly silent, cold-looking people, intent on getting from A to B and out of the chilliness of the early morning where by rights, the best place to be was bed. Clarissa couldn't blame them and paused to think how lucky she was.

But she kept on walking past the dingy ferry terminals and up the side of the Quay towards the Opera House. Once up on the terraces there, the world took on a slightly better look. The sun was finally up, the waters of the harbour, blue reflecting a clear sky, the Harbour Bridge impressive, and the Rocks area on the opposite side of Circular Quay clothed in a a pinkish light that was quite becoming.

Clarissa stood and leant on a railing fence and breathed deeply, and a movement beside her nearly made her die of fright because she'd thought she was alone on Bennelong Point beside the sails of the Opera House.

'. . . *Rob*! Oh, you gave me a fright!' she said breathlessly, staring at the tall figure of her husband, clad as she was in jeans and a blue sweater with his dark hair ruffled and a blue shadow on his jaw. 'Were you . . . did I wake you? But you didn't have to follow me. I mean I'm all right. I just felt like going for a walk.'

He smiled faintly. 'Chase you would be correct. You set a mighty pace when you go for a walk, Mrs

Randall. I thought I'd lost you a couple of times!'

'Those dark streets gave me the willies,' she told him. 'But it's rather nice up here, isn't it? Oh, Rob, you seemed to be sleeping so peacefully, and you must have been tired. I'm sorry!' she added contritely.

'No need to be,' he assured her. 'I would have been up soon, and anyway a brisk walk is a good way of getting going—to be doing it with you is a bonus.'

'You should have cooeed,' she said slowly.

He looked at her. 'You seemed to be lost in thought, Clarry. But it is nice up here, you're right.' He leant his elbows on the railing beside her and they both gazed out over the water.

Clarissa sniffed the air appreciatively. 'I feel as if I haven't seen the sea for years and years,' she said. 'In fact I can't remember the last time I did see it! It must have been . . .' She stopped abruptly.

'On our honeymoon.'

She glanced at him, but he was staring straight ahead.

'I didn't really forget,' she said uncertainly. 'I mean . . .' She bit her lip.

'Do you know what I think?' Rob said slowly. 'I think you tend to blank out the painful bits.'

'I suppose so,' she whispered. 'Although I do think of . . . they weren't all painful.'

He said nothing. Then presently he straightened and turned his back on the view, leaning back slightly with his arms folded. 'Clarry, are you ever going to forgive me and try to understand?'

She tensed and was glad they weren't facing each other. 'I have—and I do,' she said with an effort.

'Look at me and tell me that,' he said quietly.

'Rob . . .'

'Anyway, you've never let me explain, so I don't see

how you can understand, Clarry.'

'Oh, Rob,' she said tremulously, and turned towards him, forgetting she hadn't *wanted* to look at him, 'some things speak for themselves! Once I found out it was as if I'd been blind and could suddenly see everything so clearly! Like the way you looked at her sometimes and the way she'd looked at you. The times when you were tense and I couldn't understand why. I. . . I felt it too, that time you came to Sydney for Ian's birthday. I *knew* that she and my father were more and more bitterly . . . at odds. Then, at *my* eighteenth birthday party, I thought she'd invited you for my sake, but of course she hadn't. And I thought you were disturbed because I . . . because I hadn't changed . . .' She stopped painfully. 'But I know now,' she went on after a moment, 'that I probably didn't rate a second thought, not with either of you.'

'That's not true, Clarry.'

Clarissa looked away and tears shimmered in her blue-grey eyes. 'But not in the same way as you thought of her, Rob. Even if you . . . hated it, I think she must have attracted you. Do you still think of her?'

'Unfortunately I have a constant, living reminder of her,' he said drily.

'Me?'

Rob smiled bleakly. 'Who else?'

'But I'm not like her.'

'No, I didn't mean that. Shall we go back?'

Clarissa watched the Manly Ferry plough through the water below before answering. Then she didn't. She said instead, uncertainly, 'We seem to be discussing this a lot these days, don't we?'

'I don't think I've mentioned it for weeks.'

She shivered suddenly, sensing his withdrawal, and thought how remote he looked, standing tall and straight beside her now. He'd looked like that at Ian's funeral, she remembered, shut in, inaccessible—but it was more now, as if he was impatient to be gone. Yet only minutes ago he'd said something to breach the mile-wide gap that was between them despite the fact they could live together and love a child.

Or perhaps he's been saying it in other ways and I haven't been hearing it, she thought. But do I understand it any better now I have heard? Will I ever? And now he's retreating ... Out of impatience at last? Who could blame him?

'Rob,' she began urgently, but couldn't go on.

He waited for a moment or two, then turned away.

Clarissa hesitated before turning herself, then did so in a rush, saying his name again on an almost panic-stricken note. 'I ... it ... I'm *sorry*, but I just ...'

She stopped helplessly, unable to make any sense of what she was trying to say, hopelessly unsure of the chaotic emotions that possessed her—love of a kind, gratitude, but also, or still, that deep sense of hurt, of inferiority and the curious spirit of defiance that was its twin. But then again, panic ...

Which gained the upper hand and made her say confusedly, 'Don't go away from me like that. I mean ... oh, thank God!'

But those words were muffled in Rob's shoulder as he pulled her into his arms. 'Clarry, it's all right,' he said into her hair. 'I'm not going anywhere.'

'I don't mean that. I don't understand why you don't, though. Why you put up with me when I can't even be a wife!'

Rob said nothing until she had calmed down and was able to look up at him at last, her eyes wide and fearful and questioning. 'One day you might,' he told her. 'Don't worry about it in the meantime. Now, shall

we go back to Evonne before she starts to wonder if
we've absconded?'

That evening, back at Mirrabilla, Clarissa sat in the
drawing-room on her own after everyone else had
gone to bed. Rob was still in Sydney, and to do this—
sit up by herself—she'd had to adopt a line of strategy
which struck her as fairly ridiculous. She had had to
pretend she was extremely tired, because Mrs Jacobs
and Evonne had made it unsubtly clear that they
would not consider going to bed before she did.

She had regarded them fondly and exasperatedly,
and thought of telling them she was perfectly capable
of staying up on her own, not to mention perfectly fit
and able to take one late night in her stride. She'd
known, however, within a moment of the thought,
that she'd be knocking her head up against a brick
wall, so she had yawned and hidden her laughter when
they had both yawned. And she'd taken the time,
waiting in her bedroom, to ponder the fact that Mrs
Jacobs and Evonne had become unlikely allies.

She waited for half an hour, then crept out of her
bedroom into the drawing-room.

Mostly, when there was only family home, they
didn't use the drawing-room but a smaller room they
called the den, which boasted a television set and a
comfortable, rather old, leather suite.

But Mrs Jacobs had lit the drawing-room fire
tonight and shepherded Evonne and Clarissa in there
after dinner as if it was a festive occasion, and Evonne
wasn't perfectly used to the den. Mrs Jacobs'
estimation of festive occasions was a mysterious law
known only unto herself. Rob and Clarissa adhered to
it gravely.

The fire was still glowing warmly as Clarissa

wandered into the shadowed, high-ceilinged room and glanced upwards out of habit. But the new ceiling was something of a disappointment, at least to someone who had known the old so well. The mouldings weren't nearly as intricate and the pattern easy to capture, whereas before you thought you'd got its last flourish, only to find more.

She sat down in a wing-backed silk-covered chair and remembered how the builder who had renovated the homestead had suggested installing central heating. And how Rob had said it was up to her. And how she had said no, it was bad enough to have to change the ceiling.

She laid her cheek on the silk wing of the chair and thought of all the Kingstons who had known this old house, and how curious it was that she should be the last of them to bear the name—and not even do that any longer.

And with one of those odd twists of one's thought processes which leave you wondering and backtracking to find how this thought led on from the last, she saw her mother in her mind's eye. Not as she had last seen her, but in her heyday when she had been so brilliant and vibrant and lovely ... Of course the thought had been there since she had talked to Rob that morning.

An evil woman? Clarissa thought suddenly, catching her breath. No. Selfish perhaps, unthinking ... caught in an unsuitable marriage just as much as Dad ... Do I honestly believe any more that Rob was head over heels in love with her?

She moved restlessly and stared into the fire. And do I believe that he married me as a form of revenge against her? *Rob*? No ... I think she got that wrong, whatever else did happen between them. Perhaps she got it all wrong and so have I ever since. Only there had to be some reason from him to kiss her like that. But is it so important now? Whatever it was, maybe it's dead now. For him. I wonder if he's been trying to tell me that . . .

She sighed suddenly and was caught totally unaware by a feeling of regret that things had had to end this way between her and her mother. A feeling of . . .

She stood up and paced around silently for a time, trying to make sense of her feelings. Did she actually miss her mother? No, not that so much, but it all seemed a terrible *waste*, didn't it? she pondered. Three people alienated from each other in one way or another when, at least from her and Narelle's point of view, their losses should have drawn them closer together.

Clarissa sighed again eventually and went to bed.

CHAPTER SEVEN

FOR the next month life assumed a pattern that was relatively peaceful. Clarissa came and went from Mirrabilla for the series of functions that were held to mark the three-quarter centenary of Randall's, and acquitted herself well, she thought. The strikes had been averted, although narrowly, and Rob had mentioned that the spectre of them still stalked him, so she gathered that the problems hadn't been entirely resolved. And she sometimes worried about the look of strain she saw in his eyes.

In fact it was probably that, she told herself, which accounted for her new ease and fluency in socialising. A genuine desire to help him in the only way she seemed capable of. And she was a little amazed at how, with the right incentive, with determination, she was finally coping with her old bogey—shyness. I could probably have done it years ago, she thought once. Rob was right . . . But then who can say what the right incentive will be, and perhaps it is all part of growing up—especially when you're a late starter as I must have been. I bet Evonne at eighteen was quite a different proposition!

It was this thought that prompted her to mention the subject to Evonne. If anyone had told her—say on the day of Moira Stapleton's interview—that she and Evonne could achieve a rapport such as they now had, she would have rejected the idea out of hand. But now she knew she was going to miss Evonne when she left Mirrabilla, miss her straightforwardness, her intelligence, her company, the fun they had had cataloguing all the bits of history they found and the research they had started which Evonne claimed was making them authorities on the wool industry of Australia.

'Just think,' Evonne was saying that wet and windy evening, when they were ensconced in front of the den fire surrounded by memorabilia, 'it all started out with George the Third who had a strange passion for sheep, and the wife of the Spanish Ambassador to London who had a passion for matching cream carriage horses. That's how Australia eventually rose to fame and fortune on the backs of millions of sheep!'

'That's . . . stretching it a bit, isn't it?' Clarissa said with a grin.

'Not at all! And besides that, it's riveting stuff. Just imagine it—first a British fleet passes a Spanish fleet and they stop for a friendly chat during which the Spanish present the British with some merino ewes, presumably to fall back on when they run out of meat. But they don't run out of meat and the ewes make it back to England alive. Whereupon they come to the notice of Sir Joseph Banks—Captain Cook's famous botanist mate, as we were taught ad infinitum at primary school—and he decides they should be presented to the King, a keen experimental farmer. Now the King is wrapped in their fine wool as opposed to the coarser type of wool you get from English sheep, but he had a problem. No rams!'

'No?'

'No. Definitely a *no-no*, in fact, my dear Clarissa,' said Evonne, shaking her gleaming black curls vigorously. 'You see, they aren't stupid in Spain. They're doing a roaring trade in their lovely fine merino wool and they don't see why anyone else should horn in on it. Thus, it's forbidden to export rams, which the Spanish Ambassador himself, when approached on the matter, regretfully explains. All right. We now have a classic impasse.'

'We do?'

'We do. He's a man of conscience, obviously, the Spanish Ambassador. However, it comes to some crafty person's notice that his wife is—well,' Evonne raised a hand and fluttered it from side to side, 'put it this way, she has at least one weakness. She desperately covets the pair of matching cream horses that draw the King's state coach. Would she be prepared to possibly deal a death blow to Spain's stranglehold on the merino wool trade in exchange for a pair of Hanoverian matching cream carriage horses the like of which no one else has but the King, though?'

'You tell me, Evonne!' laughed Clarissa.

'The lady would, believe it or not,' Evonne said. 'So they get her her horses and she arranges—obviously bypassing the Ambassador who might have been a lot older and a doting, rather blind husband, don't you think?—but anyway, she arranges to have some merino rams smuggled out of Spain in return. Oh, Clarissa,' Evonne stood up, 'what dull times we live in! I think I'd have loved to have been the wife of the Spanish Ambassador, but I tell you what,' she said, with her dark eyes alight with mischief and mystery, 'it would have cost them a whole lot more than two horses!'

Clarissa jumped up herself. 'You would have made a wonderful Spanish Ambassadress! I can just picture you in a . . . blue velvet riding habit with your hair in ringlets under a big hat with a curving brim and a tall feather with . . . maybe a patch on your cheek and slapping your gloves gently on your knee while you bargain oh, so delicately!' She suited actions to words, pirouetting and looking out as if from beneath a large hat and holding her hands together in front of her.

'I brought you two some cocoa,' said Mrs Jacobs, appearing with a tray and looking at them askance. 'It's late and I'm going to bed,' she added in a tone of voice that suggested they might be better off there to.

Evonne and Clarissa dissolved into a fit of giggles, then Clarissa kissed her on the cheek. 'We haven't gone mad, Mrs Jacobs. And I don't suppose we'll be much later ourselves. Thank you very much!'

'She mothers you, Clarry,' said Evonne a shade enviously as she bit into an oatmeal biscuit that had come with the cocoa.

'Mmm. So what happened next in this enthralling saga? Is it true, by the way?'

'Well, it was reported in the *New South Wales Magazine* of 1883, according to C. S. W. Beam,' said Evonne. 'As to what happened next, there are two versions. I prefer the latter, but I wouldn't stake my reputation on it. Captain Macarthur bought eight of the sheep at a sale at Kew and imported them here.'

'What's the other version?'

Evonne's eyes twinkled. 'The other version is that once Captain Macarthur was here, colonising and so on, he decided there was only one way to support life in this godforsaken place, so he sent a request home for a very large quantity of rum to be shipped to the new colony, and a couple of sheep to keep his front lawn mown. But on the long sea voyage back, the message got garbled, and what he actually received eventually was a large quantity of sheep and only two casks of rum . . .'

'Ouch!' winced Clarissa, and they both laughed some more, then fell to sipping their cocoa.

'Evonne, what were you like when you were eighteen?' Clarissa asked suddenly.

Evonne raised an eyebrow. 'What's that got to do with merino sheep?'

'Nothing,' Clarissa said hastily. 'But I've found myself wondering . . .' She shrugged.

'Eighteen,' Evonne said slowly. 'I was brash, angry, determined to get out of the kind of life my mother had got herself trapped into.'

'Not shy, not . . .' Clarissa paused.

'No, although I wish now that I had been.'

Clarissa stared at her. 'Why?'

It was Evonne's turn to shrug. 'I might have saved myself some awful mistakes.'

'They couldn't have been so awful. I mean, you must have been bright and clever. Look where you are now.'

'Perhaps,' Evonne shrugged. 'But I took a few short cuts.'

'Oh. How?'

Evonne glanced at her. 'You wouldn't like to know, Clarry.'

'I would—tell me!'

'You obviously don't understand the allusion. Forget it,' Evonne said abruptly.

'Well—oh. Do you mean . . .?'

'Yes. I slept with some men to . . . further my various careers.'

'Is that how it first happened for you?' Clarissa asked quietly.

Evonne narrowed her eyes and stared into the fire. 'No, Clarry. I fell in love the first time—thought I did. I was about seventeen and a half, but I'd been working for two years and doing a night course in journalism. I *thought* I was the last word in sophistication and I

guess I couldn't wait to prove it. It—what I thought of
as the love of my life—lasted three months. *He*
obviously found it a pleasant enough interlude, but not
even serious enough to say goodbye properly.'

'What was he like?'

'Very macho, gorgeous, totally unwilling to be tied
down to a girl who'd almost fallen into his bed in her
eagerness, a girl who was too intense to have much
sense of humour ... Intense, God!' Evonne said
wryly. 'I had our whole life mapped out from the first
time he kissed me.' She grimaced, then turned to
Clarissa and blinked. 'Clarry, you're not crying for
me, are you?'

'Yes,' sniffed Clarissa.

'You're crazy, you know!'

'I know, but I like you so much. And ... and you've
been very cynical about men ever since?'

'Dear Aunt Abby,' Evonne said ruefully, 'I don't
think it's quite so simple. But don't you worry about
me, I'll survive!'

Clarissa thought for a bit with her chin propped on
her hand. 'Some people are very lucky, aren't they? I
keep thinking about the Marchmonts, for some
reason.'

'Well, they're a very striking couple.'

'And very much in love.'

'Yes. But they were divorced, you know.'

'What?' Clarissa stared at Evonne round-eyed.
'From each other?'

'Mmm. It caused a real buzz. I'm not sure how long
they'd been married before the divorce, not very long,
though—I mean a year or two. Then no sooner had the
divorce become official than they remarried. Love
must have triumphed in the end,' Evonne finished
with a slightly ironic look.

'Oh, I'm so glad!' Clarissa said fervently. 'I wonder what it was all about, though?'

'I should imagine David Marchmont could be a hard man to deal with,' Evonne said drily. 'He's certainly a hard business man.'

'I don't know much about men at all,' said Clarissa, then bit her lip and couldn't imagine what had prompted her. And not for the first time, she found herself wishing Evonne was not an employee of Rob's. Also wondering if Evonne had an inkling that all was not as it appeared on the surface between her and Rob. She must find *some* things strange, she had thought from time to time. If our positions were reversed, I know I'd at least think it strange that Robert Randall had married a girl who couldn't even go out and about without having her hand held . . .

'You don't have to know much,' she heard Evonne say slowly. 'You only have to worry about one, and I think you must know him very well!'

'Yes. Yes, I do,' she said hastily. 'Talking of . . .' She lifted her head. 'Did you hear that?'

Evonne grinned. 'You're getting as bad as Sophie, only she doesn't make mistakes. He's in Melbourne tonight, remember?'

'Then who's coming in the front door? Mem should be barking her head off!' said Clarissa in low urgent tones, and they exchanged wide glances as curiously unsteady footsteps approached down the passage.

'Clarissa,' Evonne whisperd, but Clarissa was rising stealthily. Then she stopped and stared and laughed with relief. '*Rob*! It is you! You frightened the life out of us! Rob . . .?'

'Sorry about that,' said Rob with an effort. 'I should have let you know. Hello, Evonne.' He sat down with obvious relief and reached up unsteadily to pull off his tie.

'Rob.' Clarissa was on her feet in a flash and she knelt down in front of him. 'What is it? You look terrible!' And he did—pale, exhausted and shaken, as she'd never seen him look.

'Nothing,' he said with an attempt at a smile. 'A touch of 'flu, that's all. I must have picked up Sophie's virus belatedly.'

'Then why ... Rob, you're mad! You shouldn't have been driving around the countryside in the middle of the night!'

'Only from Albury. I suddenly decided I couldn't bear to be in Melbourne, so I flew to Albury ... Clarry, don't look like that, I'm not dying. I just feel a bit crook.'

Clarissa put out a hand and touched his face. 'You should have rung, stayed put,' she whispered. 'Come to bed now. I'll get the doctor first thing in the morning.'

'I don't need a doctor,' he protested, then he did grin. 'But I won't say no to bed! Well, this is hello and goodnight, Evonne, only I might need your help in the morning. This strike thing has reared its ugly head again.'

'Forget about that,' Clarissa said as Evonne murmured something. But it did occur to her that Evonne was looking a little pale herself, suddenly. She forgot about that almost immediately, though, as she steered Rob out of the room.

'No,' she said further down the passage, 'not in there. Here.' She opened a door.

'Unless I'm hallucinating, this is your bedroom, Clarry.'

'I know,' she said, leading him in. 'And it's nice and warm, whereas yours will be cold. See, the fire's going well and Mrs Jacobs will have put a hot water bottle in the bed. Now don't argue with me about this, Rob,' she finished determinedly.

He half laughed as he stared down at her. 'No, ma'am,' he murmured, then grimaced and rubbed his temples.

'What is it?' she whispered. 'A headache?'

'Like a steel band being tightened all the time.' He looked around. 'But where will you . . .'

'Don't worry about it. I'll get your pyjamas.' Clarissa went through the interleading door and came back with them. He was sitting on the bed with his head in his hands. 'Can you manage?' she asked gently.

Rob looked up slowly and as if he was having difficulty focusing. 'Yes,' he said wearily, but she bent down and unlaced his shoes and helped him out of his jacket. The she said. 'I'm going to get you some aspirin and a hot drink.'

Evonne was hovering anxiously. 'Is he all right? I've never seen him . . . look like that.'

'Neither have I. I can't remember him ever being sick. He works too hard,' said Clarissa with sudden intensity. 'I keep telling him that!'

'What are you going to do?'

'Keep an eye on him tonight. And I'll get the doctor tomorrow, whatever he says. He might be able to talk some sense into him. You go to bed, Evonne. There's nothing you can do, and if I need help I'll wake up Mrs Jacobs. Goodnight.'

'Goodnight,' Evonne said slowly, and turned away abruptly.

Rob was in her bed when she got back with the aspirin, lying with his hand over his eyes as if the light hurt them. She switched on a lamp and doused the overhead light. 'Take these, Rob,' she said softly. He did, but seemed disinclined to drink much.

'Are you warm enough?' she asked him.

'Mmm . . . Clarry, you don't have to stay up. I'll be all right,' he said in a slurred voice.

Clarissa didn't answer but sat on the side of the bed and touched his hair lightly, then started to stroke it. He didn't say anything, but she thought he sighed. And presently he fell asleep.

She did stay up, and was glad she had, because he was restless all night, sometimes shivering, sometimes sweating with fever so that she had to change his pyjama top.

The last time she did that, she gave him some more aspirin and patiently persuaded him to drink a lemon drink she'd made, knowing it was important to keep up his fluids. But the effort seemed to exhaust him and his head sagged heavily as she put her arms around him to ease him back against the pillows.

She stopped and held him in her arms with his head on her breast—and didn't know what was happening to her. Because it was as if her whole being was suddenly concentrated on that dark head. She felt her breasts swell and her nipples harden and her womb contract. She felt suffused with tenderness and love and anxiety. She felt as if she never wanted to release him, as if life could hold no more for her than to be able to hold him like that, to soothe him and take away the pain and the strain.

'Oh, God! Oh, Rob!' she whispered with sudden tears in her eyes. She laid her cheek on his hair. 'I love you. I . . . never stopped loving you, but now it seems I love you more than ever—and as a woman. Oh, Rob, what have I done?'

If Rob heard her, he gave no indication, and she guessed he was asleep again, so she held him as close as she dared, staring over his head with wide darkened eyes at the pattern of firelight on the wall. Then, at last, as he stirred restlessly, she helped him lie back and covered him up. And when he seemed to settle, she got up and put some wood on the fire, wrenching her mind to other things. Such as whether she should ignore the fact that it was a wet, freezing night and that he was basically a strong, healthy man, and call for the doctor now. But it was a twenty-five mile drive. I'll wait, she thought. That's what Mrs Jacobs would do. The symptoms are the same as Sophie's, so it's mostly going to take care and rest.

Then it struck her that she was curiously unwilling to share this vigil with anyone, and she went back to the chair she had pulled up beside the bed and curled up in it so that she could watch him.

He seemed to be sleeping more peacefully now and she could look her fill. He looked younger as he slept, she thought, and oddly vulnerable, and she trembled with sudden longing to have him back in her arms, but he didn't stir. So she waited and watched over him until at last the rain stopped and a pale dawn came.

Then she left the room stiffly, closing the door very carefully so as not to wake him.

'You should have woken me! I can't understand why I didn't hear anything! Look at you—you look exhausted, Mrs Randall. Doesn't she, Miss Patterson?'

'Stop scolding me, Mrs Jacobs,' protested Clarissa with a grin. 'There was nothing you could have done that I couldn't. Anyway, the doctor will be here in about an hour.'

'You could have got some sleep instead of sitting up

all night. Next thing we know you'll have caught it.'

'Did you ... sit up all night?' asked Evonne, her dark eyes looking heavy as if in fact she'd been the one to sit up all night.

Clarissa shrugged and bit into her toast. 'Now don't you start fussing about me, Evonne,' she said. 'Thank heavens it's stopped raining. We sometimes have trouble getting in and out of the place after a lot of rain. Mrs Jacobs, I think we ought to keep Sophie away from Rob unless the doctor thinks it's safe,' she added.

Mrs Jacobs snorted and Sophie, who was sitting beside Clarissa dunking strips of toast into her boiled egg, asked 'Daddy sick?'

'Yes, darling. Like you were. Oh, wow! You got an egg without a face this morning. But I ...'

'I got it,' said Evonne. 'Sorry, but I didn't notice until it was too late—half eaten.'

'Neither did I—notice it,' Mrs Jacobs said shortly. 'Didn't think you'd be bothered drawing faces on eggs this morning.'

'I always draw a face on Sophie's egg,' Clarissa said mildly, and stared at Mrs Jacobs for a moment. Then she stood up and went over to her. 'Don't be cross with me,' she said softly. 'I wanted to sit up with Rob and I'm really as strong as a horse now.'

'*He* wouldn't want you to be ... overtiring yourself, Mrs Randall.'

'Then what he doesn't know can't hurt him,' Clarissa said ruefully, but she felt her heart lurch at the irony of her words.

Fortunately, perhaps, the doctor arrived then, early, which was something else that didn't please Mrs Jacobs for some reason, but it took her mind off Clarissa at least. And by the time he'd left, she seemed to have shrugged off the worst of her ill-humour.

She and Evonne were waiting in the kitchen.

'It's a type of 'flu,' Clarissa told them, having seen the doctor off. 'Complicated by the fact that he's been walking around with it for a couple of days not realising what it was—thinking he was just tired. Because he is tired and needs a break,' she added with a little catch in her voice. She turned to Evonne. 'The doctor says he needs at least a week off, but Rob seems to have other ideas, so I'm going to have to enlist your help, Evonne. He brought home a bulging briefcase which he wants to see later, he says. I want you to take it back to the office. There must be *someone* else at Randall's who can handle things, but if anything is really vital, they can ring him—in a couple of days. Evonne, you must have a fair idea what it's all about, anyway. You've helped him before.'

'Yes,' Evonne said slowly. 'I ... actually I know quite a lot about it. I also know,' she paused and looked at Clarissa searchingly, 'that there are some in top management who have always resented Mr Randall and obstructed him in various ways.'

'What do you mean? He told me some people resented him, but ...'

'I mean that they've actually fostered trouble with the unions.'

'Does Rob know this?' asked Clarissa.

Evonne smiled slightly. 'Oh yes. He's too clever not to. But it's also extremely difficult to handle.'

'I can imagine,' Clarissa said drily. She stared at Evonne. 'Would you,' she began, and stopped, then started again. 'Would you be able to sort of—keep a watchful eye over things for the next few days? I know it's asking a lot and you might not be in a position to ...'

'Spy on top management?' Evonne said softly. 'Is that what you mean?'

'Is it?' Clarissa grimaced, then said baldly, 'Yes.'

'Oh, I think I could do that. Remember the Spanish Ambassadress?'

Clarissa caught her breath. 'Yes!'

'So if I feel that things are going the way Mr Randall might not like, I'll get in touch. You can rely on me, Clarry.'

Clarissa went over to her and hugged her. 'Thanks,' she said huskily. 'I *know* he's not going to be well enough to worry about it for a while, but I also know how much it means to him. I have to thank you for so much else too. You've been the best friend I've ever had, apart from . . .'

Evonne looked deep into Clarissa's affectionate and genuinely touched blue-grey eyes, then looked away. 'The same here,' she said gruffly. 'I'll get going.'

Rob slept for most of the day and Clarissa had a sleep herself, then she went for a walk with Mem in the afternoon. They came across Holly Kingston and Clarissa spent some time handling her still gawky latest foal.

'She's a beauty,' she said to the grey mare. 'Going to be just like her mum, I reckon, and by the time Sophie's ready for a pony, she should be ready for Sophie, don't you think?'

But finally mother and foal wandered off and Clarissa leant against a gate with Mem at her feet, and found she could no longer not think about what had happened to her during the night.

'So it's happened,' she whispered, and found that her hands were shaking as she fiddled with a splinter of wood. 'How strange! Not to know yesterday, and

today to know everything. To be transformed overnight. What triggered it, I wonder? Because he was ill
and helpless? That must have been part of it, but I
think it's been coming for some time. Since we were
married? No . . .'

A bird soared overhead and she watched it with her
hand shading her eyes. The afternoon sunlight was
warm because there was no wind, and the sodden
paddocks were steaming gently.

Winter might be on its last legs, she mused, then
thought, no . . . it was quite a pure way that I loved
him then. I mean I was happy to please him, but I
would have been content just to be with him. I never
wondered what it would be like to be made love to in a
blaze of passion, in fact I was petrified to think of it. I
never longed to hold him, only to be held. I was never
posessed by this kind of hunger, this ache, this need,
this special kind of tenderness . . . I really was a child
then, in all but years, wasn't I?

The bird swooped again and she saw the white tips
of its pin feathers. And she thought of her painful
confusion lately and the odd sensations that had
affected her. Yes. It's been coming for some time, she
decided. Only *I* could have misunderstood it. I thought
I wanted to get away from him and I set out to prove to
him that I was capable of it. Then I found out that I
was doing it *for* him, but I still didn't understand.

She sighed, and Mem stirred and looked up at her.
But Clarissa didn't move. I might as well have it all out
with myself, she thought wryly, and blinked away a
tear. So I've grown up overnight, but what does that
change? All this might have happened to me in the
normal course of events and much sooner, but it
didn't. And the reason it didn't—the reason why I
went on deluding myself for so long—still stands.

Forget about my mother, she doesn't seem to matter any more. But will Rob ever see me as anything other than ... Clarry Kingston? A little girl he found he couldn't abandon ...

She laid her head on her arms on the gate suddenly, and Mem stood up and looked wistful.

'Mem, Mem,' Clarissa said brokenly. 'Oh, Mem! Nothing's changed. Only *me*, and I might have been better off the way I was. Can you imagine Rob ever looking at me the way David Marchmont looked at ...' She stopped and caught her breath as she discovered another mystery revealed to her. *That* was why the Marchmonts had made such an impression on her. It hurt to think that she and Rob didn't have what they had. Then she was struck by another thought. The Marchmonts had obviously had their problems, hadn't they? Was she being cowardly to ... give up without a fight? Was there some way she could make Rob love her ... as a woman?

She trembled and closed her eyes, going hot and cold, and knowing that understanding herself had not solved one other problem. It was all very well to feel desire, it was another thing, for her, to communicate that.

Then she straightened up, suddenly determined to *try*. After all, she had conquered other mountains for him, hadn't she?

'I've brought you a visitor, Rob,' she said three days later, from the doorway.

He was lying in her bed, staring at nothing in particular, but he turned and smiled at her, and her heart turned over as it had a habit of doing these days.

'Oh? That sounds mysterious,' he said.

'Not really,' she replied. 'But very, very impatient.'

She opened the door wider and Sophie tiptoed into the room, then raced across to the bed.

'Well, if it isn't Sophie Randall!' smiled Rob as she climbed on to the bed and he gathered her into his arms. 'How are you, sweetheart?'

Sophie was fine, she said. Sophie had missed him, she said, and hadn't wanted him to be sick so she couldn't even come and see him . . . She broke off her excited stream of chatter to glance reproachfully at Clarissa, causing her father to grimace sympathetically at her mother over her blonde curls.

And to say, some time later, when Mrs Jacobs had managed to entice Sophie away for supper, 'My poor Clarry, you've had a hard time of it these past days, I imagine.'

'Well, it wasn't easy keeping her away,' Clarissa said with a grin. 'Thank God for Clover, but I think even his ingenuity has been severely tested. Any special preferences for supper yourself?'

'No—Clarry, sit down and talk to me for a while.'

She had been absently tidying up after Sophie and she hesitated, then sat down obediently beside the bed.

'I didn't only mean Sophie,' said Rob after a moment. 'You've been such a dedicated nurse too. You've been terrific. Thank you,' he said quietly.

'It was the least I could do. And I'm so pleased to see you looking better at last,' she said lightly.

'I must say I'm relieved to be feeling better at last,' he said ruefully. 'I'm normally never sick, so it's come as a bit of a shock to the system.'

'Rob——' she began abruptly, then stopped.

'Go on.'

She looked at him and managed to say wryly, 'I was going to read you the riot act, that's all. But I think I'll leave it until . . .'

'No, don't,' he interrupted with a quizzical look.

'Well, the reason you felt so truly awful was because you've been overdoing things far too much for ages! Even the doctor said so. You need a break, a real break. I thought,' Clarissa paused and swallowed, 'I thought we might take a holiday. Would you . . . like that?' She'd said most of this to her hands, but she glanced up now and found that her heart was beating swiftly.

Rob said nothing as their gazes caught and held, and she found she was holding her breath.

'Clarry——' he stopped and sighed suddenly, and she looked away miserably, knowing what was coming, 'I can't, not just at present. Which doesn't mean to say I wouldn't like to very much. Look at me, Clarry.'

'It's all right,' she murmured. 'I understand. But I still think you should take one soon. And if you think I'm letting you leave Mirrabilla one day before the doctor decides you should, you're mistaken!' She stood up and—how, she wasn't sure afterwards—laughed down at him teasingly. 'I can also be a very bossy nurse, you know!'

For a second she saw an expression she didn't understand. Then Rob laughed himself, but said, 'Unfortunately there are some things I have to attend to now, Clarry. I was going to ask you to bring a phone in. Tomorrow I'll get up, but . . .'

'Rob,' she sat down again and stared at him nervously, 'there's something I have to tell you. You don't need to worry about work for the moment, honestly. It's all taken care of—well, so far, that is . . .' She tailed off lamely.

'Oh,' he said slowly. 'How?'

She told him, and to her amazement and then relief, Rob looked totaly stunned and then genuinely amused. But what he said jolted her. 'Well, well! I do believe I should have you on my board.'

'Not me,' she said hastily. 'Maybe Evonne because she's very clever, I think, and I *know* she has your interests at heart . . .'

'But it was your idea?'

'Well, yes. But I wouldn't have been able to do anything about it, whereas Evonne . . .'

'Is very clever,' Rob interrupted. 'So you said.'

'Don't you agree?'

'Yes.'

'And she's rung me every day. Of course I know she can't hold the fort for ever, but . . . oh, Rob, you must spend a few more days recuperating,' Clarissa finished with an odd little break in her voice.

'You're very concerned for me, Clarry, aren't you?' he said at last.

She got up and walked over to the window. 'There's no reason why I shouldn't be, is there?' she mumbled, but in her mind she was saying to herself, tell him—say it now, it's the perfect opportunity! But the words wouldn't come. In fact it was worse, for she found herself adopting a falsely bright expression then and swinging around with a glance at her watch to tell him it was time to take the pills the doctor had prescribed.

He did, without comment, and she left him for a while, but with her heart as heavy as lead.

Altogether Rob stayed home for just over a week, though, to Sophie's great and Clarissa's secret joy. Nor did he seem restless, and they spent some time with Cory Kessels inspecting the sheep and the improvements that had been recently finished on the shearing shed.

'It's good to be home,' Rob said idly one afternoon as they walked their horses back towards the homestead. It was a week to the day since he had arrived home so ill.

'It's good to have you home,' she said huskily. 'Almost like old times.'

'Clarry . . .'

'But we're having an early dinner tonight,' she interrupted, not knowing what he had been going to say but afraid for some reason.

'I'm quite all right now,' he observed.

'It's not that. It's a surprise,' she said mysteriously.

He frowned. 'Company?'

'No. Oh no! But I'm not going to tell you any more. You'll just have to wait and see!'

They had arrived back at the stables. Rob slid off his horse and before Clarissa got a chance to do likewise, he reached up and lifted her down with his hands about her waist. 'I could make you, you know,' he said softly, still holding her. 'Tell me, I mean.'

'No, you couldn't,' she whispered.

'That's really tempting me!'

'You . . . you——' she stammered, colouring and looking up at him uncertainly, 'I'd rather you didn't. I mean, I'd really like it to be a surprise . . .' She tailed off, biting her lip, and Rob stared down into her eyes, then let her go rather abruptly. But he said mildly, 'Okay, so be it,' and turned away to his horse.

Clarissa cursed herself inwardly through the rest of the afternoon, and through dinner, for having let another opportunity slip through her fingers.

The surprise was *Horizons*, and Clarissa hadn't even told Mrs Jacobs that she'd received a note from Moira

Stapleton telling her about the screening date, although she had mentioned it to Evonne on the phone.

But she knew she had puzzled Mrs Jacobs with a request for an early dinner, and it took some artful manoeuvring to have her in the den as she switched the television on, right on time.

Rob was already there with Sophie on his knee clutching a story book, and with his coffee beside him.

The screen lit up to the sound of the clip-clop of horses' hooves, and a lone horseman came into view, shadowed against a brilliant backdrop of sky and tall, waving golden winter grass. Then the horse stopped and the rider turned back and a dog hove into view and another camera focused on the rider so that you could see it was a girl with long hair, but still there was no sound apart from the dog panting, and it came to a halt and looked up at the rider. The frame was frozen for a moment and Clarissa remembered with a curious prickling of her skin how it had happened. How Mem had played her part so well as if she'd known she was on camera . . .

Then the screen came alive with swirling dust and a river of sheep, and Clarissa and Cory riding as if they were part of their horses, Mem leaping and barking, and crawling on her belly, sheep bleating and turning and looking as they always did, comically bewildered, then bunching . . . A close-up of Clarissa whistling, then a startling cut to Clarissa seated in the drawing-room with Sophie on her lap and from then on a montage of Clarissa, sheep, the shearing shed, Mirrabilla and in the background, while the titles came on, *Click go the shears, boys, click, click, click* . . . that old song being sung and played in the background.

While Sophie stared at the screen, her blue eyes round with wonder, Rob sat up alertly and Mrs Jacobs sank down into a chair open-mouthed.

And as Moira Stapleton's cultured voice came on, they all turned accusingly to Clarissa and she smiled feebly. 'Thought I'd surprise you,' she said.

'You have,' Mrs Jacobs said. Then, 'Shh . . . I don't want to miss a word!'

Rob winked across at Clarissa over Sophie's head and reached out to take her hand.

It was a curious business, Clarissa decided, seeing yourself on television. It was like looking at a stranger in a way, because your mannerisms, that you knew you possessed but were largely unconscious of, were suddenly there. Like the way she often chewed the corner of her lip before she spoke. But the biggest surprise of all was how poised she had been, and how natural.

In fact that was what Mrs Jacobs said as the last shots were fading and Sophie was standing excitedly in front of the television saying, 'Sophie!' as she had for each of her appearances . . . 'A born natural, I reckon you are, Mrs Randall—a born natural! Why haven't we got one of those new-fangled videos? We should have taped that!'

'She said she was sending me a tape,' Clarissa murmured, still staring at the screen, at the three of them, herself, Rob and Sophie, standing on the verandah. Then the screen was blank, and Clarissa slowly turned her head to Rob, to find him already looking at her.

'That was very well done, Mrs Randall,' he said.

'Well, I thought the camera work was wonderful!' Clarissa rushed into speech. 'And . . .'

'No, you were, Clarry. Without you, they wouldn't

have had a programme.'

Clarissa blushed. 'Do you think so?' she asked tremulously.

'I know so. I . . .' Rob stopped as if choosing his words with care, 'I hope that demonstrates to *you* that you're capable of so much now, Clarry.'

'I . . . it surprises me,' she whispered, and neither of them noticed that Mrs Jacobs had removed Sophie to the kitchen with the promise of milk and a bedtime snack. 'It's as if the . . . inner me and the outer one,' she shrugged, 'don't know each other very well sometimes, don't match. Does that make sense?'

He smiled faintly. 'We all have our inner fears and insecurities,' he said. 'But if you weren't coping with them, you wouldn't have been able to do that so well, and so much more these days. I'm really proud of you, my Clarry,' he said.

Clarissa looked down and thought with breath-taking suddenness of the times, most of her life in fact, when to hear him say that had meant more to her than the world. But now it didn't do that, it chilled her slightly, and she knew exactly why. Because it implied so much, that she was still in essence a child to him, still growing up, still in need of praise and encouragement, still perhaps an emotional invalid—maybe coming out of it, but fragile and delicate . . . If only he'd said I love you, Clarry, she thought, if *only* . . . But then isn't it up to me now to let him know that's what I want to hear? What's holding me back like this? Why can't I just say the words? Because I'm afraid to find out he *doesn't* love me . . .

'Clarry, what is it?'

She took a breath. 'Rob, I . . . ' But the phone that was switched through to the den rang shrilly and they both jumped.

'I'll get it,' she said, and got up.

It was Evonne, sounding urgent. 'Clarry, is that you? Can I speak to . . .'

'Yes, he's here, Evonne,' Clarissa cut in. 'Has something come up?'

'Yes, that only he can handle now. Clarry, I didn't get to watch the programme, but I set my video to record it. How was it?'

'Fine. I'll give you Rob.'

Rob put the phone down five minutes later with a frown and his mouth set in grim lines.

'Is . . . it's serious,' Clarissa said.

'Yes. I'll have to go back.'

'Not tonight, Rob . . .'

'No, but first thing in the morning. I'll do what I can on the phone in the meantime . . .' He stopped and looked at her rather penetratingly. 'Sorry your surprise had to end up like this.' He put out a hand and took her chin in his fingers. 'What were you just about to say to me?'

Her eyes widened and she opened her mouth, then closed it. 'Nothing important,' she said instead. 'It will keep.'

'I'd rather it didn't.'

Clarissa stared up at him, knowing that look in his blue eyes only too well. 'I . . .' she licked her lips, 'I was only going to say that I know I . . . that you were right about me even up until . . . well, only a few weeks ago, probably. But I *do* realise now that I can cope and that I can put it all behind me. Do you . . . do you believe me?'

His very blue eyes narrowed consideringly and his fingers moved on her chin, then he dropped his hand suddenly but didn't answer.

'You said just now—you said yourself,' she hesitated, 'that I must be coming right. At least, I think that's what you meant.'

A nerve moved in his jaw. 'What do you want to do about it, Clarry?' His words were curiously clipped.

'Nothing ... not anything ... particular,' she replied unfluently. 'Not tonight, anyway. I know ...'

But the phone rang again and Rob swore and picked it up, then curtly told whoever was on the other end to hang on.

Clarissa stared at the receiver in his hand and swallowed, then she looked up at his face which was still slightly pale but scored now with harsh lines. And she couldn't help herself, she reached up and touched his cheek, 'Just don't worry about me, I guess that's all I'm trying to say. You've got more than enough to worry about now, Rob,' she said lightly. 'Look, I'll go and pack for you so that you can go first thing in the morning.'

'Clarry ...'

'No, Rob,' she smiled up at him, 'that's all, I promise. Forget about it. You'd better answer that.' And she walked away.

But she cried herself to sleep, because she was such a coward. Although in the morning she was up bright and early and by a tremendous effort of will, able to present a perfectly normal, not-a-care-in-the-world image.

Rob still said to her by way of parting and with a lurking smile in his eyes, 'Don't do anything I wouldn't, Clarissa Jane.'

'No, Rob.'

'I'll be at the Regent, by the way, same suite. As for you, Sophie Randall, take care of your mum.'

Sophie threw her arms around his neck, and as usual, shed a few tears as the car disappeared down the driveway. But this time her mother cried with her, nor were Clarissa's tears as easily stopped as Sophie's —not those in her heart, anyway.

For the rest of the morning Clarissa was gripped by a restlessness that would not be stilled, and a loneliness such as she had never known.

So although she wasn't expecting anyone and didn't recognise the large limousine that sailed up the drive after lunch like a liner, anything to take her mind off herself seemed like welcome relief.

But when she saw who emerged from it, her mouth fell open and her heart started to race, and Mrs Jacobs, who happened to be helping her re-pot some plants on the verandah, dropped her trowel and an earthenware pot that splintered into shards. She also exclaimed, 'My God . . .'

But the other person to emerge from the limousine came up the steps first with his hand outstretched and said, 'Well, little lady, you must be Clarissa Jane. How do you do? I've brought you a visitor.'

CHAPTER EIGHT

'MUM' breathed Clarissa, and started down the steps.

'C-Clarissa,' Narelle said shakily, her face pale and anguished, 'don't turn me away, *please*!'

'Now she's not going to do that, Narelle,' the man said soothingly with a decided American accent. He turned back to Clarissa and smiled at her, and with a jolt, Clarissa realised that this was her stepfather, and that he was tall and broad and muscular, that he had rather humorous brown eyes set in an ugly, tanned face, and very big hands ... at least, at first impression he was ugly, then there seemed to be something irresistibly genuine about him.

'I ... no, of course ... oh, Mum!' Clarissa said shakily. 'I have missed you!'

'Darling,' Narelle said tearfully, a little later, 'I have to explain, still. Will you let me do that? I won't rest easy until I do, and Wenden knows that. That's why, last night when we quite accidentally saw you on television, he said afterwards, I think she might be ready to understand now. That's why he bullied me into coming—I really wouldn't have had the courage to do it on my own. That's why he's charmed Mrs Jacobs into arranging a tour of the property for him, while I do. Will you,' her lips trembled, 'will you let me, Clarissa?'

'Mum ...'

'It ... it can only be what you want to hear,' her mother said. 'Rob *never* even liked me, let alone anything else. Nor had anything ever happened between us, I swear, until that night. Apart from,' she stopped and sighed, 'some flirting on my part which started out like a game, really. I mean, by the time he was twenty, it was obvious he would wreak havoc with women. But all he ever accorded *me* was an ever-growing cold, silent disgust which I deserved, but if you can imagine what kind of a goad that was! I was also . . . I think when you get to your thirties you start to worry about growing old and unattractive, and your father and I . . . oh, Clarissa, we were such opposites!'

Clarissa acknowledged this silently.

'Then, when Bernard died,' Narelle went on, 'I suddenly found myself in the position of virtually having nothing. And I hadn't seen Rob for ages, believe me, until your eighteenth birthday party. Well, I don't suppose I have to tell you what it was like. But for me it was a revelation—here was a man amongst men, here was Rob as I'd known—without ever knowing about Robert T.—he would be one day. Mature, powerful, everything a woman could wish for. I . . . I persuaded myself that I was in love with him, that I even had a prior claim on him, that it *could* work, especially in this day and age. That our age difference needn't matter. I told myself that that cold silence of earlier years had probably been shyness and . . . and confusion because of Bernard and Ian . . .'

'Go on,' whispered Clarissa.

'So I . . . I thought the best thing I could do was cut my ties with Mirrabilla, something I didn't appear to have much choice about anyway, provide for you as well as I could and—start again. Then,' Narelle's voice shook, 'he married you. I couldn't believe it at first. But as soon as I *had* to, I started to rationalise it. I told myself that he'd been in love with me all those years, long before *I* had taken it seriously, and this was his revenge for—for the way I'd toyed with him and teased him and ...' She stopped and looked at Clarissa despairingly.

'Oh, Mum,' Clarissa sighed, 'don't ...'

'I must. Clarissa, I could blame it on—well, mid-life crisis is a good enough term, I suppose, and it certainly wasn't easy for me. But it was more than that. I'd become so used to thinking only of myself—I had no idea what I'd become. But that night when you overheard what you did and saw what you did, I have to tell you that it was one of the most humiliating experiences of my life, and I now have a few to choose from. And not only because of you, but because of the way Rob kissed me ... It wasn't out of suppressed desire, it was an act of ... as if he was saying—there, you've been panting for this long enough ... '

Clarissa made a distressed sound.

Narelle said, 'I don't suppose Rob's shown you that side of him, because he loves you, but most men possess it. It's the ultimate male form of,' she shrugged, 'contempt for a woman. And I finally began to see how worthy of it I was.'

'Because of me?'

Narelle closed her eyes briefly. 'That's what started it. Even if I never showed it much, I loved you, Clarissa. I just had no idea how much, or what a lousy mother I'd been, until ... until we revived you and you looked at me out of your father's eyes, and I knew what I'd done.

'Wenden,' she went on after a time, during which Clarissa had slid her hand impulsively into hers, 'completed the process. After Rob had repeatedly refused to let me see you again, I went a little berserk, I guess. I took up the old social whirl, I really threw myself into it, believe it or not. I met Wenden at a party—he has investments in Australia and comes here often—and I found I kept on meeting him. Then one day I got drunk and he rescued me from ... circumstances I wouldn't like to describe to you, and he sobered me up and told me to my face that I was a worthless, drunken lush, an incredibly vain middle-aged bitch with no prospects other than a career of enticing young men into my toils, and, he suspected, a closet full of unbearable memories. I ... I broke down and told him everything. He said, well, you can't turn back the clock, but if you can't learn from your mistakes you might as well give up. Then he mentioned that he happened to love me in spite of all my faults and would I care to marry him. So I did, because I couldn't think of anything else to do. Then one day I woke up and discovered that I'd fallen in love for the first time in my life.'

'I'm so glad,' said Clarissa with tears in her eyes.

'I suppose,' Narelle went on blinking too, 'you're wondering why I needed to tell you all this. It's obvious you and Rob have sorted it out between yourselves. I saw that last night—you looked so lovely and poised and happy. But I've been haunted ever since, and always will be a little, by that terrible look in your eyes and ...'

'Mum ... Mum,' Clarissa said softly, 'it's over now. And there's someone I'd like you to meet. She was taking her nap, but I hear sounds!'

'Well,' observed Mrs Jacobs as the limousine disappeared down the drive, 'I must say I liked him, and I think he's just what your mother needs. What will you tell Mr Randall? Do you think they knew he wouldn't be here?'

'No. I think they'd have come anyway, Mrs Jacobs. I think Wenden C. Whittaker has large and not unfounded confidence in his ability to work miracles. That's what Mum said, and I agree with her. I liked him very much too.'

'You didn't answer my question,' Mrs Jacobs said softly. 'My other one.'

Clarissa took a breath. 'My mother thinks ... everything is all right between me and Rob. She just *assumed* that from seeing me on that television programme. I didn't tell her that it's not, because I'd already stopped blaming her for ... oh, Mrs Jacobs, I'm in trouble!'

'Miss Clarissa,' Mrs Jacobs said unsteadily, calling her that for the first time for years, 'do you think I don't know that? Do you think I haven't seen you waking up like a flower to loving him and not knowing what to do about it? Why do you think I've been so grumpy lately?'

'You ... you have,' Clarissa agreed tremulously. 'Is it because you think I'm a fool not to let him know?'

'No. It's because I know you're afraid to get hurt again, and I've wanted to help but couldn't. See, no one can, really. Not your mother, not me, although,' Mrs Jacobs added just a little drily, 'she might have looked just a bit closer. But that's her, and leopards don't change their spots ...'

'She *has* changed a lot,' Clarissa pointed out.

'I know, and I give her credit for it.' Mrs Jacobs grimaced. 'Anyway, I always liked to think I did more for you than she did. So don't take any notice of me, Miss Clarissa ...'

'Oh, Mrs Jacobs!' Clarissa put her arms around her and hugged her. 'Do you know, *I* don't know what I would have done without you.'

Mrs Jacobs hugged her back fiercely and briefly. 'Or him,' she said.

'Yes . . .'

'Then you must know he'd never do anything to hurt you!'

'Yes, but that's the problem . . .'

'Now look here,' Mrs Jacobs said sternly, 'just ask yourself *why* he wouldn't ever do anything to hurt you. And keep asking yourself that question all the way to Sydney, tomorrow, first thing.'

Clarissa stared at her. 'But . . . but,' she stammered, 'he's so busy. He's got all this to worry about, this strike . . .'

'And you can keep making excuses for the rest of your life, Mrs Randall!'

'Oh, don't call me that!'

'But that's what you are, after all.'

'I . . . all right. You're right,' said Clarissa, and kissed Mrs Jacobs impulsively.

'Kiss Sophie too?' a little voice piped up.

'Oh, of course!' Clarissa picked her up. 'How many?'

'Ten times ten and another ten!' Sophie said, but was quite content with ten.

Sydney or the bush? Clarissa thought the next morning, rather humourlessly considering her state of controlled nerves, as Clover drove her to Albury where she took a flight to Sydney.

In fact Sydney was basking in late winter sunshine when she arrived. She took a taxi from the airport to the Regent, and at Reception was just about to ask for a key to the suite when she stopped and, instead, booked a room. Then she was immediately fearful that she would be recognised and would be causing some speculation, but the girl behind the counter checked her computer and said that yes, they did have a room for her, and if the name Randall meant anything to her, she showed no sign of it.

Once in the room several floors below the suite, Clarissa sank down on to the bed and asked herself if this was a further delaying tactic or what.

Well, he won't be there *now* anyway, and I'd rather . . . surprise him, she told herself. She reached for the phone and asked to be connected with Mr Robert Randall. The reply came swiftly that Mr Randall was not in and not expected back until seven.

'There, you see,' she muttered to herself as she put the phone down. 'It just means that I've got the afternoon to get ready.'

She picked up the phone again and made an appointment in the beauty salon for later, ordered lunch and after it, lay down on the bed. But she didn't sleep. She found herself thinking instead of Western Samoa and her honeymoon.

Some hours later, she stared out over the lights of Sydney, and tried to gather courage. She was wearing a blue silk dress which Rob had once said he liked, her hair had been done and shone and rippled, her make-up was minimal but perfect — and her hands were shaking.

She turned and stared at herself in the mirror and the image that stared back at her was poised and groomed but also young and slender, and very grave.

But I can't help being young, she thought. Nor can I help being nervous—yet I can't go on for the rest of my life hiding behind it. No.

The suite was three floors up, and the possibility that Rob would be dining out was one Clarissa had taken into consideration. If he was, she would have to come back later, because it seemed curiously important to retain the element of surprise—and she suddenly realised why. It could be a yardstick to measure his reaction by.

She stepped out of the lift and automatically turned right, her footsteps deadened in the thick carpet. She knew from habit that the suite was three doors down from the lift, but she had only passed the first door when Rob's door opened and a dark-haired woman came out. Clarissa took a few more silent steps then stopped dead.

It was Evonne, standing outside Rob's door with her hand behind her, still on the handle. Then she dropped her hand and brought it up to her face as she leant back against the door.

It was Evonne who stood like that for a moment so still with her head back so that her pale, lovely throat was exposed. It was Evonne who moved presently and wearily, to brush a hand over her hair, then smooth the skirt of her elegant turquoise suit and check the buttons of her navy-blue blouse ... Evonne, presenting an unconscious picture of sensuality and totally unaware that Clarissa stood only feet away, rooted to the spot.

Then she straightened and turned fully towards Clarissa—and gasped. A dark tide of colour flooded her throat and her cheeks and her lips stayed parted in horror.

Clarissa blinked, and like a kaleidoscope once again fragemented incidents, words, looks—all whirled in her mind, to settle finally into an unmistakable pattern. But what was worse, perhaps, was the knowledge that that once vaguely held suspicion about Evonne and Rob had been so ... cleverly? ... yes, cleverly lulled. Because they certainly hadn't been blatant.

Could I be forgiven for being fooled? she wondered as she stood in the middle of the passage still rooted to the spot. Or was I only blind and incredibly naïve? But I'm certainly not blind now. Even I can read guilt like Evonne's . . .

She swallowed and suddenly came to life, turning swiftly and stumbling back towards the lift.

'Clarissa !' Evonne was beside her, saying her name desperately, but Clarissa ignored her and stepped into the lift which was still waiting on the floor. Evonne got in too.

'Please, let me explain,' she said breathlessly. 'You don't understand . . . Don't look like that!'

'I do, I do,' Clarissa whispered.

'No! You can't possibly. Where—what——' Evonne said disjointedly as the lift stopped three floors down and Clarissa stepped out. 'Where are you going? Are you staying here?'

'Unfortunately, yes.' Clarissa slid her key into the lock. 'Evonne,' she turned to the other girl, 'there's nothing we can say to each other. Don't you understand? It's better left—but just one thing. I don't want Rob to know I was here, that's all.'

'Clarissa, you've got to let me explain,' Evonne begged, and her throat worked as she tried to go on. 'It's not what . . . it's . . .'

'But you love him,' Clarissa broke in with sudden intensity. 'I saw . . . I'm not blind any more. And once I saw, I understood so much more. Why you looked so pale the night he came home sick—a hundred little things. It's really happened for you this time, hasn't it?'

'No ...'

Clarissa turned away abruptly.

Evonne took a tortured breath. 'All right, *yes,* God help me,' she said anguishedly. 'But ...'

'E-Evonne,' Clarissa broke in raggedly, 'for what it's worth, I can't blame you—either. I even thought once how good you would be for him, and I'm sure it was obvious I was not a good wife, not even really a wife. But if you could just do this for me. If ... the time we spent together meant anything to you, please do as I ask.' And she took advantage of Evonne's confusion to slip inside and close the door firmly. It locked automatically.

Evonne knocked and kept knocking on and off, discreetly, for about five minutes. Then there was silence for a quarter of an hour until the phone rang, but Clarissa ignored that too.

In fact she barely heard it as she desperately tried to bring her emotions under control, but the pain and the hurt was so great she could only shake uncontrollably until she forced herself to drink some brandy.

It occurred to her that this time she wasn't going to be able to blank anything out. This time she was going to suffer the pain to the fullest, and she wondered bleakly if it was a mark of maturity.

Then she sat down on the bed and wondered what to do. Go home? But the thought of it seemed monumental, and anyway, if Evonne did tell Rob, did it matter where she was?

'No,' she whispered, 'I might as well stay here for the night. I'll go back in the morning.'

She forced herself to take a soothing bath, but new tears came as she picked up her dress from the foot of the bed and hung it up. I left it too late, she thought. Years too late. And she buried her face in the blue silk and wept again, for the fool she was and because she had no idea what to do next.

She fell asleep, finally, long after midnight, somewhat reassured that Evonne had at least bowed to her request.

When she woke, it was after seven and there had been nothing to disturb her sleep. But she was concerned that she'd slept late—the earlier she left, the less chance she had of running into Rob or Evonne. Perhaps I'm best to wait a while now, she mused. And to take her mind off things, she rang up and ordered breakfast.

While she waited, she donned her robe and brushed her hair and washed her face, then started to pack.

She sent up a brief prayer that it was only breakfast when a knock came, which it was, but with Rob about two paces behind it.

There was nothing she could do but stand aside and let the waiter wheel the breakfast trolley in.

Rob's blue eyes met hers briefly, then he motioned her in and followed, and they stood silently as the waiter fussed around the trolley, propping up the folding leaves and removing plates from the warming compartment, also uttering cheerful remarks about the weather, until finally he looked at them in turn, uncertainly, and left awkwardly.

'Well, Clarry?' said Rob at last, his blue, blue gaze flickering over her from head to toe and coming back to rest interrogatively on her pale face.

She stared at him, then shrugged helplessly.

'What's that supposed to mean?' he queried.

'I . . . nothing,' she said huskily, and bit her lip.

'Nothing?' he repeated softly but somehow menacingly.

She shivered inwardly and thought dazedly that it was Robert Randall standing across the room from her, someone she hardly knew, tall, good-looking, remote—and angry. Because I've found out? she wondered dully. But he couldn't have expected to keep me in the dark forever . . .

She swallowed and licked her lips. 'Evonne told you,' she whispered. 'I asked her not to.'

'That was very kind of you, Clarry,' he said grimly, 'but we'll deal with Evonne later. I want to know why you were here in the first place. *Now*.'

'I . . . it . . . there's no reason why I shouldn't be, is . . . there?' she stammered. 'I'm not supposed to be a prisoner. Am I?'

'Oh no,' said Rob with irony. 'That was your idea,' he added, and she flinched visibly, but he went on, 'Does this visit by any chance have anything to do with a certain conversation we had a couple of nights ago?' he asked, and skirted the breakfast trolley to come to stand right in front of her.

Clarissa raised scared, uncomprehending blue-grey eyes to his.

'Does it, Clarry?' His voice flicked her like a whip.

'I don't know what you mean . . .' She took a frightened step back and tried to turn away, but he took her by the shoulders and swung her back. 'Wh-what conversation?' she faltered as his fingers dug into her flesh beneath her robe. 'Rob, you're hurting me!' she whispered.

He let her go abruptly. 'The one we had about how well and fit you are now,' he said sardonically. 'Well enough to strike out on your own, perhaps? Is that what you were trying to tell me? But obviously you didn't think I'd believe you, or so I'm left to wonder. Did you decide then to come down and gather some

ammunition with which to end our marriage? Is that
it?' He waited for a moment with his mouth set in a
hard line while Clarissa stood in stunned, incredulous
silence. Then he went on remorselessly and with an
unpleasant smile, 'Well, you can have it from the
horse's mouth, my dear. No, I haven't lived like a
monk for the past two years. I've strayed from time to
time while you lived in your own little world which you
were so loath to leave. Nor do I particularly commend
myself for it, but perhaps I'm only human. *Nor* can I
recommend it to anyone, but perhaps I can say in my
defence that it was only ever bought and paid for in
one way or another, and never worth the spiritual
distaste it left me with. But I waited for you for a long
time, Clarry.'

Clarissa closed her eyes. 'I didn't come to *spy* on
you.'

'Then *why* ? Why the separate room, the sneaking
around?'

'I . . . is that all Evonne is to you?' she whispered,
her lashes fluttering up and sticking wetly together.

'Evonne doesn't enter into this,' he said harshly.
'Just as your bloody mother never did, only you could
never understand that, could you?'

'No . . . yes . . .'

But he overrode her as if she hadn't spoken, as if he
hadn't heard or as if her miserable confusion had
finally tested his patience too far. 'Well, I'm going to
tell you exactly how it was with your mother, Clarry.
At first I couldn't believe her . . . such subtle
innuendoes, I thought I was imagining them. Then I
got out and about in the world and saw enough to
understand that it was possible. And for a time she
held a sort of fatal fascination for me, even though I
could only despise her—she was very beautiful.

Nineteen, twenty and twenty-one aren't the easiest years for *anyone*, Clarry, and to be under that kind of ... siege—well, put it this way, I sometimes just couldn't help thinking—and wondering. But that was *all* it was, and anyway it was always tinged with a sense of disgust. Then the disgust got the upper hand, or perhaps I just grew out of certain fancies that plague very young men,' he said drily. Then his mouth hardened again. 'As for that night . . .'

'I know, I *know* . You don't have to,' Clarissa broke in hoarsely, 'explain.'

'No, you don't. You know nothing, Clarry. But the time has come to make you understand—I'm sorry it has to be this way, I told myself it never would again, but *something* has to get through to you.' he said with a sort of naked savagery, and pulled her roughly into his arms.

'Rob!' she breathed, but he only bent his head to seek her lips with his. 'Rob . . . oh, please . . . I . . . '

'Shut up, Clarry,' he muttered against her mouth. 'I'm not going to hurt you.'

But he did.

Although, during what followed, Clarissa knew it was partly her fault that he was hurting her. She was so stiff and awkward, so stunned and shocked, and unable to believe it was happening or know why it was happening, let alone able to unravel the paradox that existed within her. Because in spite of everything, it was what she'd longed for, wasn't it? Since the night she'd nursed him and come to understand what she felt for him.

But all the same, she was as unprepared for it—as hopeless—as she'd been the very first time.

Then it was over abruptly. Rob rolled away from her, breathing heavily, and leaving her crying quietly.

'Don't,' he said huskily, after minutes had ticked by.

Clarissa tried to say something, but the words got stuck in her throat. He sat up suddenly and stared down at her wordlessly, then closed his eyes briefly and pulled the sheet up over her naked body and lifted her bodily into his lap. 'Are you all right?' he asked, smoothing her tangled hair.

'Y-yes . . .'

'No, tell me honestly. That couldn't have been pleasant for you, but it's also been a long time.' He stared down at her searchingly.

She licked her salty lips. 'I . . . I'll be all right. I'm sorry . . .'

'*You're* sorry,' muttered Rob almost under his breath, and held her close for a moment. 'Clarry,' he said then, 'I think you're right. I think the time might have come to . . . make some changes.'

She moved convulsively, but he wouldn't let her leave his arms. 'Not right this minute,' he murmured. 'Relax, rest for a while—all day if you like. I just wish there was someone—you shouldn't *be* here like this!' he added his voice suddenly sharp with frustration.

Clarissa winced inwardly. 'I could go home later,' she whispered.

'Could you,' he hesitated, 'would you be . . . no, I've a better idea. Come.'

'Are we going somewhere?'

'Yes. Upstairs. Not the best place perhaps, but better than this.'

'Rob, I don't want to . . .'

'All the same you will. There's no one up there. I'll just get dressed. Have you got a coat you could slip on over your nightgown?'

They heard the phone ringing as Rob slid his key into the lock of the suite, and he swore softly.

'That's what I meant,' he said grimly. But he sat her down in a chair before he answered it. And from the brief conversation he had, she gathered it was his secretary, and from the curt instructions he issued, she realised he was instructing her to come to the hotel because he wouldn't be going to the office. Then he put the phone down, only to pick it up again straight away to tell the switchboard to request all callers for him to ring back in half an hour.

'Now,' he said, turning to Clarissa and smiling briefly, but his smile died and he crossed the room swiftly. 'Oh God, Clarry, don't look like that . . . not so tragic,' he said urgently, pulling her to her feet and taking her into his arms, 'We'll work something out.'

She swam up, hours later, from the depths of sleep, and lay quite still for ages, listening to the muted sounds coming from the sitting-room. Quiet voices that she couldn't distinguish, a door closing, the telephone.

I couldn't have chosen a worse time for this, she thought. But perhaps there was never a right time.

A tear trickled down the side of her face into her hair and she turned at last to bury her face in the pillow. But she couldn't bury the memories. So, after a time, she got up and wandered into the marble bathroom.

Rob had asked her if she would like a bath, but she'd only looked at him dazedly and he had put her to bed as if she was a child, as if she was Sophie, and sat beside her stroking her hair. She had fallen asleep quite quickly.

Now she sat on the edge of the bath as the water

flowed in, and trailed her fingers in it. Then she turned the taps off and stood up restlessly. She slipped her nightgown off and slid into the warm depths. A curious thought slid across her mind—was that being made love to in a blaze of passion, or was it what my mother spoke of? An act of contempt . . . An act of *impatience*, purely male because I'm so dumb, because he's—he *was*—determined to make a go of this marriage for reasons I don't understand. Yes, I do . . . did, she corrected herself. Sophie. He's always made it quite clear he wouldn't let her go. Is that what he meant before . . . it happened, about getting through to me and making me understand? Only now I think he's changed his mind. And who could blame him? I was so *wooden*, so useless.

She closed her eyes, but couldn't shut the images that swam behind her eyelids. And she discovered with despair that it hurt her much more to think that Rob was finally prepared to end their marriage than to remember his summary possession of her body. It was a bitter ache within her to think that she had failed totally to communicate with him, in spite of all the periphery complications like his complete misunderstanding of why she was there in the first place, such as Evonne . . .

'I should have told him,' she murmured out aloud, and sat up agitatedly. 'I should have told him the plain truth, *somehow*. That even if I am hopeless in bed, I *love* him. That I don't care about the Evonnes . . . why didn't I understand that before? He was right, they don't enter into it, but how ironic that he should have said that.'

Have I left it too late? she asked herself after a time. Did I . . . he did say he'd waited for me. He also said something about a spiritual distaste. But then for anyone with principles it's probably a distasteful position to be in. A wife who deludes herself into thinking she doesn't want you and then when she discovers differently, can't show you or tell you. But then that's assuming that a wife is all you would want or need in the first place, and *that's* been something I've never been sure of. That's been the crux of my incredible turmoil, Rob . . .

'It's just a pity,' she whispered, 'that I should have found out too late that I want you on any terms. That I would give my whole life to be able to relive this morning, because there must have been some way I could have shown you . . .'

CHAPTER NINE

WHEN Clarissa finally got out of her bath, she discovered that her things had been brought up from downstairs while she had slept, so she dressed in a cream linen skirt, a wattle-yellow shirt and a cream sleeveless pullover. She added matching yellow pumps and sat for a long time brushing her hair before she tied it back with a yellow ribbon. She could still hear sounds from the sitting-room, but it seemed to her that there was only one voice—a female voice, talking sporadically into the phone, she guessed.

Finally, after pacing around restlessly, she decided she couldn't hide for ever, even if Rob was out there, so she took a deep breath and opened the door and walked through.

A middle-aged, grey-haired woman turned from the table she sat at immediately, and got up with a warm smile.

'Why, Mrs Randall,' she said. 'How do you do? I'm Molly Reynolds, Mr Randall's private secretary. I thought you might be up, because I heard the bath. I do hope you're feeling better? Mr Randall said you'd been a little unwell this morning. He also asked me to tell you that things had reached a flashpoint and he was forced to go out, but that he will definitely be back for dinner.'

Clarrissa blinked, then smiled and took Molly Reynolds' outstretched hand. 'How do you do? I . . . I'm fine now, thank you. There's no need . . . I mean, if you're here because of me it's no longer . . .'

'Well, I am, and happy to be so,' Molly Reynolds interrupted. 'It's much more peaceful here than in the office. Now, if you're feeling better, would you like a spot of lunch?'

'Well——' Clarissa began helplessly, forming the distinct impression that she wasn't going to be able to budge Rob's secretary, and remembering suddenly that he'd told her once his private secretary was a lady of great value to him—serene, unflappable, immovable when she chose. 'Well, yes, now you come to mention it,' she said, recalling also that she had missed dinner last night and breakfast this morning. She smiled at the unsinkable Molly. 'But only if you'd care to share it with me, unless you've already had yours?'

'No, I haven't. Let's consult the menu!'

Incredibly, Clarissa sometimes thought afterwards, she spent the rest of that day being alternately charmed and cosseted by a stranger.

Molly Reynolds had been Robert T. Randall's private secretary before he died and she had a store of fond anecdotes about him . . . 'A real old tartar he could be, but we loved him,' she said several times.

'I know Clover was very close to him,' Clarissa said once. 'He's told me so . . .'

'Oh, dear old Clover!' smiled Molly 'How is he?' This brought forth some more serious stories. And all the while Clarissa gathered that young Mr Randall had carved his own niche in Molly Reynolds' heart. 'A chip off the old block,' she said of him, approvingly. And, 'He'll sort this mess out—he's just been waiting for the right opportunity to strike. His grandfather was a master of the right timing too, you know!'

After they had lunched, Molly suggested watching a film on television, so they consulted the list and chose a comedy and, to Clarissa's amazement, thoroughly enjoyed it together. Amazement, because she didn't understand how she could be enjoying anything, and amazement that their senses of humour should coincide so well.

The earlier stream of phone calls seemed to have dried up. Then when they were having a cup of tea, and the sun was starting to set, the phone did ring.

Molly answered it and said almost immediately, 'Yes, Mr Randall . . . yes, fine . . . well, congratulations, if I may say so. Yes, I will. Yes, I'll be here.' And she put the phone down and beamed at Clarissa.

'Is it over?' Clarissa asked.

'It certainly is, Mrs Randall. Believe it or not, it was a member of the board of directors who was actively encouraging unrest amongst the union delegates. I think we all had our suspicions, but it was very hard to prove. He . . . resented your husband right from the beginning, I'm sad to say. But now he's been exposed and he's resigned. I just wish Miss Patterson was here to share the good news, since she had a hand in exposing him.'

'E-Evonne . . . where is she?' Clarissa asked a little unsteadily.

'Of course, you know her, don't you? Well, apparently some urgent personal business came up out of the blue and *she* resigned, very early this morning, so Mr Randall told me. A shame, really, but these things happen. Once I got to know her, which took some doing, mind, I got to like her and she was extremely efficient. Mr Randall will miss that. He'll be back soon, by the way,' she added warmly. 'Still feeling all right?' she asked then.

'Yes. Yes, I'm fine,' Clarissa said quietly.

Rob came not long afterwards.

He thanked Molly Reynolds not only for today but for her loyalty to him and to Randall's. Whereupon Molly dabbed away a tear and told him that it was her pleasure. Then she surprised Clarissa by hugging her and finally she left, enjoining them to relax and celebrate.

Shadows were falling across the room as the door closed behind her. Rob stood by the phone table and Clarissa stood beside the chair she'd risen from when he'd come in.

The silence lengthened with the shadows as they stared across at each other, Clarissa with her heart hurting because Rob looked tired and drained, the line of his shoulders weary yet tense beneath his dark suit, his eyes impossible to read.

'I'll get you a drink,' she said huskily at last. 'You look as if you could do with one. I'm ... I'm very happy that it's all been cleared up, happy for you.'

But she didn't move immediately, because his eyes didn't leave her face and she wondered, suddenly, if he had even heard her.

She licked her lips and was about to say his name, but his lashes lowered abruptly and when they lifted, that fixed look had gone from his eyes. He said, quite normally, 'Thank you, Clarry. Yes, I could do with a drink—several, possibly. Have one yourself.'

She poured two Scotches, which she didn't normally drink, but she had the awful feeling she was going to need something strong. When she carried Rob's over to him, he had pulled off his tie but was still standing beside the table. 'Why don't you sit down?' she suggested.

'Just now,' he murmured, and took the glass from her.

Clarissa hesitated, then took her drink over to the chair she had vacated and sank down into it. 'Here's to Randall's,' she said, raising the glass. 'I should have opened some champagne! How silly . . .' She stopped and bit her lip, realising that her voice had sounded high and unnatural.

'Don't,' said Rob quietly, not looking at her.

'Don't what?' she whispered.

He stared down at his glass. 'We don't have to make conversation. Clarry, this morning at the height of the mayhem, I got a phonecall from Wenden C. Whittaker.'

Clarissa made an inarticulate sound and he looked at her briefly. 'It came as something of a surprise,' he went on. 'He said that both he and your mother felt they owed me an explanation, that it was not his way to go over people's heads or behind their backs. That they'd not known whether I'd be at Mirrabilla when they came—in other words, they hadn't been avoiding me—but that *he* had taken it upon himself to decide there wouldn't be another opportunity as good . . . for you and your mother to make up your differences. He said the fact that he'd been right didn't alter, in his judgement, the need to explain the matter to me. All of which rather floored me . . .'

'I wanted to tell you, Rob,' Clarissa broke in.

'I know—I didn't give you much chance,' he said with something like distaste, and drank some Scotch. 'So you've forgiven her, Clarry? She said you had and told me that you'd acquitted me of . . . my part in the affair some time ago.'

'You spoke to h-her?' Clarissa stammered.

'Yes,' he said briefly, then went on, 'I'm not sure it was what either of us really wanted, but Wenden C. is a very persuasive person.'

'I liked him, Rob,' Clarissa said tremulously. 'I liked him very much, actually. And she's really in love with him. I think they'll make it.'

'What did she tell you?'

'What you told me last night,' Clarissa said slowly. 'But more.'

'And you told her you'd ... already worked it all out?' he queried.

'No,' she said honestly. 'She assumed that, but she was right, I had.'

There was silence for a time. Clarissa hadn't tasted her drink, but some instinct made her take a sip of it now, because she felt suddenly more afraid than she'd felt all day.

Rob said at last, 'Then it only leaves Evonne to be explained now, doesn't it?'

She stared at him with parted lips, but he wasn't looking at her. She swallowed. 'Rob, I don't have to have Evonne explained, and anyway, you must be tired and ... it's not the time for this.'

'There's never going to be a better time, Clarry,' he said drily, and walked over the the window.

She stared at his back and held her breath until he turned abruptly. 'Evonne came to see me very early this morning,' he said without preamble. 'She looked as if she'd been up all night—she said she had. She looked cold and pinched and desperately worried—and at first, after I'd let her in, as if she didn't know how to begin. Then she stood behind that chair you're sitting in and told me baldly that she'd fallen in love with me.'

Clarissa moved and clenched her hands together.

He watched her hands for a moment, then raised his eyes to her face. 'I have to tell you, Clarry,' he said quietly, 'that it came like a bolt from the blue to me. I don't know whether you'll believe that, but it's true. No, let me go on,' he said as she parted her lips to speak. 'Evonne then said that she'd never intended me to know and wouldn't be telling me then, if it weren't the only way to explain what had happened.' He shrugged. 'I couldn't help admiring her, Clarry. It isn't the easiest thing to do, to have to confess to something like that when you know it's not reciprocated. To have to explain that there are times when it's so hard to hide what you feel, but you go on doing it because the other option, of going away, is almost unbearable, because just being near ... that someone is enough, you tell yourself. To have to explain,' he said quietly, 'that she had stood outside my door last night after a perfectly legitimate business meeting and for a few moments, let her guard right down.'

'Oh God,' whispered Clarissa, and fought back the tears.

'She then,' Rob went on, 'explained about you and how you'd obviously misunderstood, although she couldn't blame you for that. How you'd asked her not to tell me, not knowing that I'd be the last to know. But how she couldn't bear to have you think that of her, and me, apart from the fact that she was so worried about you. That she'd spent the whole night racking her brains for a solution, for a way to make you listen to her and believe her—and in the end, had known that this was the only way. But not to know,' he said wearily, 'that it didn't really matter, for us.'

'Rob,' Clarissa breathed, 'of course ... why are you telling me if ... you're *angry* with me because I didn't trust you!' she finished agonisedly and disjointedly. 'But ...'

'I told you,' he interrupted, 'for Evonne's sake. It seemed to mean a great deal to her, it must have for her to have put herself through that and to insist on resigning there and then, although—that was inevitable. I told you for *your* sake, Clarry. I know how much you'd come to like Evonne. I . . .' he stopped abruptly. 'Perhaps you're right, though. Did you *honestly* believe I'd foist someone I was sleeping with on to you like that?'

Clarissa stared at him. 'I . . . oh, Rob,' she said painfully, 'I didn't know what to think. But you see, I think *I'd* always known she was in love with you. Even so I got to love her and care about her as if she was a sister. I'll miss her.' She put her hands to her face because the tears were brimming.

'Will you miss me, Clarry?'

Clarissa went still and wondered frantically for a moment if she had imagined those softly spoken words. But as her hands dropped to her lap, she stared straight into Rob's eyes in the last of the daylight, and knew with a sickening lurch of her heart that she hadn't.

She stumbled up and ran across to him. 'No! Rob, no— not *you*! Please, oh, please, not you . . .'

He put his drink down and caught her in his arms. 'I couldn't *stand* it,' she gasped. 'I'm sorry for everything!'

'Clarry, Clarry,' he said gently with his arms just lightly around her shaking body, 'yes, you *can* stand it. You're a big girl now, you don't need me as a prop any more. In fact I think you know that better than anyone. This—is just reaction, habit.'

She went still again and lifted her face to his. 'What do you mean?' she asked fearfully.

Rob hesitated briefly. Then he said with an oddly twisted smile, 'I think you came here yesterday to tell me something. I know I accused you of—other things, but in retrospect, I think it was to tell me, to really make me believe you'd grown up. Wasn't it?'

'*Yes*, but . . .'

'Well, I believe you,' he said. 'I also know now you won't be on your own without me.'

'I *will* . . .'

'No, Clarry,' he said steadily. 'Your mother and . . . this must be a day for momentous decisions,' he lifted his eyebrows wryly, 'but your mother and Wenden have decided to live in Australia now. They'd been thinking of it for some time, but they finally decided this morning. They told me they'd like to see as much of you and Sophie as possible—it appears that Wenden C. Whittaker has no children and was much taken with you two. *You've* told me you really liked him and I formed the impression that you might be right, but more—that he might be the one to bring out the best in your mother. And they'll be there for you, Clarry. You won't need me.'

'Sophie . . . this will break Sophie's *heart*.'

'Sophie is only two,' he said on a suddenly harsh note. 'Young enough to get over it. But I'd like not to lose touch with her completely. We could work something out.'

'Work something . . . oh,' Clarissa said vaguely, and when Rob dropped his arms from around her, she stood wavering like a young tree in a storm. Then she took hold and said despairingly, 'I was right—I was right all along. You never did love me, Rob. You were my safe harbour and now you're passing me on to the next one.'

'Clarry . . .'

'Rob, if you could do one more thing for me—tell me the truth. For so long now I've not known what to think. Did you ever . . . this morning, no.' She started to cry silently. 'It doesn't matter.'

'What about this morning?' he said presently in a strained voice. 'Tell me.'

She couldn't, though.

'Clarry, you should try and forget about this morning.'

'But I never will,' she whispered. 'However hard I try.'

Rob closed his eyes briefly and said, 'Don't. I'm sorry, I never meant it to happen.'

Clarissa took a breath. 'Because you ...' She stopped and swallowed. 'I won't forget,' she said softly, 'because all day today I was hoping that what happened might have happened ... in a ... a ... blaze of passion for you.' Her last words were barely audible.

Rob stared down into her pale face, then turned away abruptly. 'It did, unfortunately,' he said.

'Rob,' her heart seemed to have stopped beating, 'then why are you sending me away? Is it because ...'

'Clarry,' he swung round, 'look, I thought I could wait. I found out this morning that I can't ... guarantee it any more. And anyway,' the suppressed violence left his voice, 'it's never going to happen, which is not your fault, so don't start worrying about that,' he smiled at her tiredly.

'That ... that I'm never going to be any good in bed?' Clarissa voice shook. 'Is that what you found out?'

He stared at her, then said roughly, 'That's got nothing to do with it. What the hell are you talking about?'

She made a tired, defeated little gesture. 'I think it has. We might have managed otherwise, mightn't we?'

Rob made an exasperated, impatient sound and suddenly grasped her shoulders in a grip that hurt. 'If you're basing your estimation of your ability in bed on this *morning* . . .'

'Why not?' she cried, finding herself in the grip of something more than his hard hands—anguish and mental torment. 'I only ever came to Sydney to . . . to tell you that it was what I wanted to do . . . Rob, you're *hurting* me!'

He let her go and she noticed that he was breathing heavily. 'Are you trying to tell me,' he shot at her, 'that you came here to seduce me?'

'No. Yes.' She coloured and tried to look away, but he wouldn't let her. 'Well, to tell you,' she whispered, 'that I thought I might have fallen in love with you— as distinct from having loved you all my life.'

'And what made you think that?' he asked unsteadily.

'It was the way I felt—feel. It's . . . just there inside me.'

They stared into each other's eyes. Clarissa swallowed and forced herself to go on. 'I came to tell you that, but f-first there was Evonne,' she said tearfully, 'then you were so angry with me and then there was *me*. Really hopeless again . . . but I've been trying to tell you for weeks.'

'Oh God,' he said quietly. 'And now I've done this. Clarry,' he reached for her and gathered her close, 'I've been trying to tell you and show you for years the very same thing. I know, I know,' he said softly, 'why you didn't want to listen, why you couldn't understand—but don't you see, what happened this morning was the culmination of loving you and wanting you for so long and being desperately afraid I was losing you.'

She stood quite still in the shelter of his arms and raised stunned eyes to his. 'I thought—oh, Rob . . .'

'When did this happen?' he interrupted. 'This miracle,' he added with a smile growing at the back of his eyes. 'Did it happen suddenly?'

'Yes—no—well, it did in a way,' said Clarissa disjointedly. 'But I think it had been coming for a long time, only I was too stupid and stubborn and wrapped up in myself to see or understand.' Her lips trembled.

'And when did this all hit you?'

'The night you came home so ill.'

'I wondered once whether I shouldn't inflict some damage on myself!' he said with a grin.

'Rob . . .' Her eyes were pleading.

He raised his hands and cupped her face. Then he picked her up and took her over to the settee to sit down with her in his lap. 'Darling . . .'

But she gripped his hand urgently. 'Rob, I didn't know . . . I'm so different . . . I couldn't really believe I was what you . . .' She stopped helplessly.

'What I wanted?'

'Well, yes. Even when I sorted everything else out *that* . . . was what I couldn't understand.'

'Because you're so different?' His eyes glinted.

'I am, aren't I?' Clarissa said unhappily, and tensed as Rob took a ragged breath but pulled her closer.

'Yes, you are,' he said in a husky undertone. 'So different, and that's one of the reasons why I love you so much—and want you very much too. I told you this morning that I could buy . . . some physical release,' he said a little drily. 'But I could never *buy* you. You gave me your love and affection when I'd done nothing to earn it other than be a friend. You gave me your trust and admiration long before I found I was getting it wholesale—and not the genuine article either. And all the time you were growing up like a flower unfolding before my eyes. Tender, lovely, true . . . but so young.'

'Too young?' she asked gravely.

'Not now. But then, yes. And so I said to myself, wait. Let her spread her wings a little. Wait, because what she feels for you might only be part of her growing-up process and heightened anyway because she often didn't have anyone else to turn to. Wait until that adolescent crush, so innocent, becomes something more. Then fate forced my hand. But that might not have mattered in time, if . . . well . . .' He stopped and sighed.

'Oh, Rob!' said Clarissa, and buried her face in his shoulder.

'Clarry—look at me,' he said after a moment. And when her eyes met his, he went on, 'Being good in bed—which seems to worry you so much—is several things. Some people achieve it quite easily and enjoy it for itself. Other people find that it's a matter of mental communication as well and can't get it right if all is not well in that area, or find it just doesn't mean very much to them if there isn't *more* to it. And then there's an awareness of it that comes to different people at different stages. I think,' he searched her face, 'it's come to you now, whereas before it hadn't really.'

'Yes,' she said tremulously, 'but . . .'

'Hang on, let me finish. Let's take one thing at a time,' said Rob gently. 'However it's happened for you has never had any bearing on the attraction you've held for me—on the way I've handled it, perhaps, but not the basic thing. You see, men fall in love with who they fall in love with. Women too. But I can assure you I'm not the only man in the world to fall in love with someone young and innocent. A lot of us do. I'm really not a freak, you know.'

Clarissa had to laugh, although shakily. And she rested against him holding his hand.

'Do you need more proof?' Rob asked softly.

'No . . .' But she got it.

'When,' he paused briefly, 'Evonne said what she did to me this morning, I found I knew exactly what she was talking about—why you stay when you know there's no hope, why you just can't take that final step until something happens that you bitterly regret, and I'll always regret what I did to you this morning. Other things,' he went on after a while. 'Do you remember all the times you told me I worked too hard? Well, it was either that or . . .'

'Oh, Rob!' she breathed guiltily, and on an impulse sat up a little and kissed him. And when he responded very gently, a rush of warmth flooded her—and more. All the sensations that had plagued her lately together with the yearning, aching tenderness she had experienced once before that had been such a revelation to her.

Until finally she lay flushed and dishevelled in his arms. 'How . . . how was that for a late starter?' she whispered.

'You know what they say about late starters?' murmured Rob with a glinting smile growing in his eyes. 'Once they get going, they find it hard to stop.'

'Oh, I hope so,' she said, then blushed and trembled and buried her face in his shoulder.

CHAPTER TEN

'TIME really flies!' smiled Clarissa. 'I can't believe Sophie's three tomorrow.'

She was wearing an ivory satin nightgown that clung to her body beneath a violet velvet robe as she sat in front of the dressing table brushing her hair. Winter was in the air and she thought that from tomorrow she would ask Clover to set fires in the bedrooms, and that she would get out everyone's warm nightwear. Not that ...

She glanced at the bed to find Rob watching her. And from the way he was watching her, she new exactly what was going to happen to her once she slid beneath the sheets next to him. But the miracle was that she could look forward to it now with shy anticipation, that she could love in return ... even sometimes with what she thought was astonishing boldness.

Thinking of it right then seemed to produce the spirit of it within, so that she turned away and put her brush down slowly. She stood up and fiddled with the sash of her robe for a moment, then let it slide down her body to lie in a rich heap of colour on the floor. She stepped delicately away from it and lifted her hands to push out her hair from the back of her neck, then she stayed still with her arms raised as her hair billowed, then sank in a shining cloud. And she turned fully towards the bed and lowered her hands slowly so that the ivory satin which had tautened over her breasts so that her nipples were clearly outlined loosened a fraction.

Then she bent down gracefully and lifted up the hem and whisked it off over her head. Only she froze a little then with the lamplight gleaming on her skin, and her eyes suddenly shocked at her incredible . . . wantonness?

But Rob moved at last and said in a low husky voice, 'Come here, my little witch.'

She went in a flurry of arms and legs, dropping the nightgown and slipping under the covers and into his arms, where she buried her head in his chest and found that her heart was beating most unnaturally.

Rob said, 'I hope you mean to go on.'

Clarissa turned her face slightly but her voice was still muffled. 'Go on?'

'Mmm. I rather thought you were planning to make love to me in a . . . a *blaze* of passion.'

'I think I was. Do you mind?' She was still clinging to him rather frantically.

'Not really,' he said, and she winced at the amusement in his voice. 'Considering,' he added, easing her away from him so that he could look into her eyes and sliding one hand through her hair and the other lingeringly over her bottom, 'that that is exactly what I had in mind for you. But what went wrong?'

Clarissa lay in his arms and considered, herself. She thought of the nights, the long, lonely nights she had spent in his bed, and how all that had changed now, and how she sometimes felt she just couldn't contain the love she felt for him, it was so great.

'Nothing went wrong,' she whispered. 'Just my silly inhibitions having . . .'

'I love your inhibitions,' Rob interrupted softly against her throat.

'Oh! Well, I was going to say that they were having

a final twitch, but if . . .'

'I love the thought of that too,' he interrupted again.

'Does that make sense?' Clarissa enquired demurely.

'Possibly not,' he conceded, his mouth sliding down towards her breasts. 'Do we have to make sense, or should we make love instead?'

'Do I have a choice?'

'I see what you mean about your inhibitions,' he said, raising his head. 'In fact I can see that right now you're looking very cheeky and positively smug—for someone who was so afraid they would never be any good in bed. And I shall have to do something about that.'

'Well, I'm ready and waiting,' Clarissa said innocently, and wound her arms around his neck. 'In fact *I'm* dying slowly inside, of the unrequited desire to be *very* good in bed!'

'Show me, then . . .'

She did, with love, some tears of joy and laughter, although she had a lot of help.

Nine months, three days and seven hours later, Sophie Randall's brother made his hurried entry into the world, causing Dr Forbes to say sternly, 'Now, now, young man, I'm all for a bit of alacrity in these matters, but there's no need to gallop!'

To which admonition he received a lusty, unaided yell in return.

And Clarissa, gazing down at her new, dark-haired, definitely cross, impatient-looking son, thought with a leap of her heart—Ian. And Rob, though. I was going to call him Ian, but . . .

It was Sophie who settled the matter. She climbed on to her mother's bed some time later, was given her new brother to hold and gazed down at him with obvious delight—and incidentally, he stopped crying immediately—then she said definitely, 'I'm going to call him him Billy.'

'Well,' Rob grinned across at Clarissa, 'that solves that!'

'William,' Clarissa said slowly. 'William Randall, that's good! William Ian . . . Bernard Peter Randall— but I wanted to put in Robert too!' she said perplexedly.

'William Ian will do,' Rob said firmly. 'We'll have to keep some family names for other sons anyway.'

'Oh, now you tell me!'

But later again, when Sophie had been very reluctantly consigned into Mrs Jacobs' care and William Randall consigned to the nursery, Rob firmly closed the door of the private room, locked it and came back to the bed, where he lay down beside Clarissa, although on top of the covers, and took her into his arms.

'Is this allowed?' she asked softly.

'I don't care if it's not,' he replied. 'Do you?'

'No. I love you.'

He held her gently, and she loved that too, because it seemed to infuse strength and warmth into her weary, slightly battered body. 'I think he's going to be a handful,' she murmured drowsily. 'He has that look about him, William Ian Randall does. But you know, although I might want to wait a while, we could have as many children as you wanted. We could . . . start a dynasty. Would you like that, Rob?'

'Clarry, are you trying to tell me something?' he queried as he stroked her hair.

She hesitated, not sure how to put into words what

she was thinking. 'I wondered once what it was you were seeking in life, Rob,' she said slowly, not sure that he would understand.

But he did, because he said after a long time, 'You were right to wonder. Because I didn't know myself. Now I do and you're right again. Nothing seemed ultimately . . . satisfying, I guess, because I lacked a sense of identity, of family. But it's *you* who have given me that, along with a son and daughter. And if you want to have more children I'll be only too happy to oblige,' he added with a glint of laughter in his blue eyes. Then he sobered and looked down at her lingeringly. 'Just don't ever forget that it all revolves around you, though. That you are the heart of the matter, in other words, my darling Clarry,' he said, and kissed her deeply.

Six exciting series for you every month... from Harlequin

Harlequin Romance·
The series that started it all

Tender, captivating and heartwarming...
love stories that sweep you off to faraway places
and delight you with the magic of love.

◆

Harlequin Presents·
Powerful contemporary love stories...as individual as the women who read them

The No. 1 romance series...
exciting love stories for you, the woman of today...
a rare blend of passion and dramatic realism.

◆

Harlequin Superromance®
It's more than romance... it's Harlequin Superromance

A sophisticated, contemporary romance-fiction
series, providing you with a longer,
more involving read...a richer mix of complex plots,
realism and adventure.

Harlequin
American Romance™
Harlequin celebrates the American woman...

...by offering you romance stories written about American women, by American women for American women. This series offers you contemporary romances uniquely North American in flavor and appeal.

◆

Harlequin Temptation™
Passionate stories for today's woman

An exciting series of sensual, mature stories of love...dilemmas, choices, resolutions... all contemporary issues dealt with in a true-to-life fashion by some of your favorite authors.

◆

Harlequin Intrigue
Because romance can be quite an adventure

Harlequin Intrigue, an innovative series that blends the romance you expect... with the unexpected. Each story has an added element of intrigue that provides a new twist to the Harlequin tradition of romance excellence.

Harlequin Books

PROD-A-2

What the press says about Harlequin romance fiction...

"When it comes to romantic novels...
Harlequin is the indisputable king."
—*New York Times*

"...always with an upbeat, happy ending."
—*San Francisco Chronicle*

"Women have come to trust these
stories about contemporary people,
set in exciting foreign places."
—*Best Sellers*, New York

"The most popular reading matter of
American women today."
— *Detroit News*

"...a work of art."
— *Globe & Mail*, Toronto